LOVE DRAWN you Like a Sister

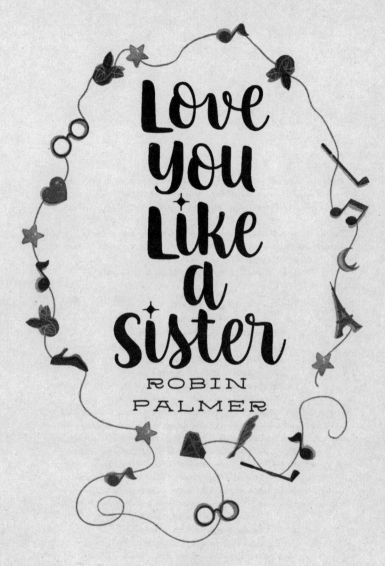

Love
you
Like
a
Sister

ROBIN
PALMER

m!x

ALADDIN M!X

NEW YORK LONDON TORONTO SYDNEY NEW DELHI

This book is a work of fiction. Any references to historical events, real people, or real
places are used fictitiously. Other names, characters, places, and events are products
of the author's imagination, and any resemblance to actual events or
places or persons, living or dead, is entirely coincidental.

ALADDIN M!X

Simon & Schuster Children's Publishing Division

1230 Avenue of the Americas, New York, New York 10020

First Aladdin M!X edition May 2017

Text copyright © 2017 by Simon & Schuster, Inc.

Cover illustration copyright © 2017 by Lissy Marlin

Also available in an Aladdin hardcover edition.

All rights reserved, including the right of reproduction in whole or in part in any form.

ALADDIN and related logo are registered trademarks of Simon & Schuster, Inc.

ALADDIN M!X and related logo are registered trademarks of Simon & Schuster, Inc.

For information about special discounts for bulk purchases, please contact
Simon & Schuster Special Sales at 1-866-506-1949 or business@simonandschuster.com.

The Simon & Schuster Speakers Bureau can bring authors to your live event.

For more information or to book an event contact the Simon & Schuster
Speakers Bureau at 1-866-248-3049 or visit our website at www.simonspeakers.com.

Cover designed by Karin Paprocki

Interior designed by Mike Rosamilia

The text of this book was set in Palatino LT Std.

Manufactured in the United States of America 0417 OFF

2 4 6 8 10 9 7 5 3 1

Library of Congress Control Number 2016947406

ISBN 978-1-4814-6643-1 (hc)

ISBN 978-1-4814-6642-4 (pbk)

ISBN 978-1-4814-6644-8 (eBook)

Love you like a sister

one

♥

I had no idea when I woke up that Saturday morning that it would go on to be known in my diary as TDIAC.

TDIAC is short for "The Day It All Changed." While I don't think of myself as a lazy person, writing out "The Day It All Changed" can be pretty time consuming. And I can think of a lot better ways to spend my time—like going through Pinterest and Etsy for inspiration for my jewelry line that I have. I'm a jewelry designer. The name of my company is Avery Lynn. (Lynn is my middle name.)

A lot of the jewelry designers I admire use their

first and middle names for the names of their companies, so I do as well. Luckily, I have a jewelry-designer-sounding name. Unlike, say, my friend Mary Helen O'Donahue.

The day started like most Saturdays did—with my mom stumbling around the kitchen mumbling, "How could I have forgotten to fill the coffeemaker again?" while I went through the garage sale section of Craigslist and came up with a list of ones for us to hit before everything good was gone. Since it was July, there were a lot of them. Summer was a good time to have them, because the weather was good.

Professional garage salers got there a lot earlier than we did—even before the official start time. But because I was dependent on someone who couldn't drive without first having her coffee, I'd have to wait until I had my license to become one of those.

I had inherited my love of vintage stuff from my mom. But while she headed toward the racks of clothes when we got to a sale, I hit the tables where all the random odds and ends were: buttons, felt flowers that had fallen off hats, earrings that were missing their mates. Because most of that stuff was pretty useless, it wasn't expensive, which meant that I could end up going home with a lot. Which, for a businesswoman like myself, was helpful. I might have been only twelve and going into seventh grade, but I had already made fifty dollars in profits over the last year.

Sometimes, just to make conversation, the person having the garage sale would ask me what I planned to do with the stuff I was buying, but I always played dumb and said, "I'm not sure yet."

But of course I *did* know—I was going to use it as part of a piece of jewelry. All of my pieces were made from found objects—that was my thing. I was afraid if people knew the real reason, they'd charge me more. Plus, it wasn't a *total* lie—most of the time I wasn't *exactly* sure what I was going to use it for.

"Those people in the white house with the red door on Wisteria are having another estate sale," I announced. Mom always said that an estate sale was the same as a garage sale, except people thought they could get away with charging more when they called it that.

From behind me I heard the skittering of coffee beans on the floor. Not only couldn't my mother drive before having her coffee, she couldn't see, either.

"Can we go?" I asked.

"Mm," she grunted, which was Early Morning–ese for "yes."

The last time we had been there, I had found a bag of twenty-five antique-looking Chinese coins that I got for five dollars. I put them on leather cords to make chokers, and when I wore one to school, my teacher, Ms. Fournette, said it looked like something you'd see in *Lucky* magazine, which I took as a huge compliment. I gave her one for Teacher Appreciation Week, and she wore it a bunch of times.

I got so excited about garage sales that I wondered if I had inherited it from my dad as well. I made a mental note to put it on my TTAMDNTISH list. TTAMDNTISH stands for "Things to Ask My Dad Next Time I See Him," which is also somewhat time consuming to write out.

Because I barely ever saw him, the list tended to be on the long side. My parents had gotten divorced when

I was two, and for most of my life he had been living across the country in California. He e-mailed me on my birthday and holidays (well, two holidays—Christmas and Thanksgiving), and if he happened to be in New York for work, he'd take me to dinner, but that happened only about once a year.

"Mom?"

"Mm," she grunted. Obviously the coffee wasn't ready yet.

"Does Dad like garage sales too?" I asked. Sometimes when the list got really long (which it was at the moment because I hadn't seen my father in one year, four months, and twelve days), I asked her the questions. Otherwise I'd never get through the list when I saw him, especially because he always asked for the check before I was even done with my meal.

The puttering behind me stopped. "I don't know," she replied, suddenly sounding awake. "Why?"

I turned toward her and shrugged. "No reason, really," I replied. "Just wondering."

Now that I had brought it up, I wished I could take it back. Mom got really weird whenever I brought up my dad. She'd answer my questions, but I could tell from the way her voice got all high, like my music teacher Mrs. Malone's, that it wasn't her favorite subject. I did know, however, that every time she looked at me, she felt like she was looking at him. At least, that's what I heard her tell her best friend, Maggie, a while back. It was kind of crazy how much I looked like him. Same stick-straight caramel-brown hair. Same blue eyes. Same heart-shaped face. Mom, on the other hand, was the opposite: curly blond hair, green eyes, super tall. No one could believe we were related, even though she had, like, a billion framed photos of when she was pregnant with me around the house.

At least she didn't say mean things about him in front of me, like my best friend Lexi's mom did about her dad. If you ask me, it was totally unfair to do that to a kid, especially a kid like Lexi, who tended to cry at commercials, especially ones about families getting together for holidays. But no one bothered to ask me, so I just kept quiet about that. I didn't even tell Lexi, and we told each other everything.

Mom came over and took my face in her hands. "Have I told you yet today how much I love you?"

"Nope. You haven't said anything because you haven't had your coffee yet," I replied.

The freckles on her nose scrunched up as she smiled. It was like looking at my own face, except for the freckles. I wished I had some. "Well, I'm telling you now. Can you add it to the list of previous 'I love yous,' please?"

I smiled back. "Done."

"How many does that make?" she asked.

This was one of the bazillion different routines we had. Sometimes I rolled my eyes and told her she was being corny, but the truth was I secretly loved it. "At least one for every day I've been alive."

"Good. And you'll let me know if I miss a day?"

I nodded. "I will."

She leaned in and kissed me on the forehead. "I'm counting on that."

"Mom?"

"What is it, lovebug?"

"You need to brush your teeth."

She laughed. "I love that I can always count on you for the truth."

It was slim pickings by the time we got to the house on Wisteria with the red door. From the looks of it, whoever lived there was big into fishing and boats, because most of the stuff left behind was in the shape of a fish or a boat. Unfortunately, other than a stuffed animal in the shape of a monkey, which might have made a cool purse with the stuffing taken out and a strap sewn on, there was nothing all that interesting left. And when I examined the monkey more closely, I saw that he was missing an eye, which kind of creeped me out.

Mom, on the other hand, was psyched, because she found a caftan to add to her collection. A caftan is a long, flowy robe-type thing that women (and some men) wear in countries in the Middle East and Africa. She loved them because they were what she called "boho," which was short for "bohemian," which meant "usually very colorful and somewhat weird." I guess you could say that my style was on the boho side as well. My boho-ness was more like fuchsia cotton shirts with embroidery and beads from a store called India Fashions in Queens near my grandparents' apartment. Which was what I was wearing that day, underneath overalls, with a pair of yellow Havaianas flip-flops. I definitely had the colorful thing down.

Luckily, there was another garage sale nearby, a few blocks over on Gardenia. The town where we lived in New York had an area called the Garden District, where all the streets were named after flowers. We lived on Tulip Drive, which made sense for me, seeing that tulips were my favorite flower.

As we walked up the driveway, I could tell I had hit the jackpot. It was like craft central, with everything from easels to glue guns to a Maxwell House coffee can full of beads. I was particularly excited about the box of paintbrushes I found for two bucks. I needed brushes for Painting Pals, which was this weekly get-together at an art gallery in town on Wednesday nights that me and Lexi liked to go to. Our latest project was a painting of a dorse. When I told Mom about it, she squinted her eyes, so that her freckles scrunched up even more, and tilted her head like she always did when she was confused, because she had no idea what a dorse was. No one did, on account of the fact that Lexi and I had made it up. A dorse was an animal that had the body of a horse and the head of a dog. Lexi was better at drawing than I was, so she drew it, and I was in charge of filling it with paint because I had a steadier hand and better concentration and therefore stayed within the lines.

I pulled out my iPhone, which I had gotten from my grandparents for Christmas, so I could text Lexi and tell her.

major score @ garage sale, I typed. I wasn't a fan of capital letters, so I always typed in lowercase. Except for school stuff—then I used them. Otherwise I would have had points taken off my grade.

BARRETTES?!?!?!? Lexi immediately typed back. She was addicted to her smartphone and had it with her at all times. She even used to take it with her into the bathroom, but after she dropped it in the toilet and had to get a new one, she stopped doing that. She was also what Mom once called an "enthusiastic communicator," which explained why she used extra punctuation and lots of caps even when she wasn't yelling. Lexi was also on a barrette kick. Unfortunately, they weren't a big garage sale item.

nope. paintbrushes! I typed, adding an excited emoji. I was a big emoji user. Sometimes when I didn't feel like doing my homework, I'd dream up new ones. Last week I was all excited because I had come up with a yoga one, which was a person sitting with her legs crossed and her eyes closed, meditating. But when I Googled "yoga emoji," I found out someone had beat me to it. At least I knew I was on the right track.

Oh. Well, can you see if they also have BARRETTES????

already checked. negative.

Well, YOU'RE A GREAT FRIEND for checking!!!!!!!!!

thx. gotta go. call you when i get home. I loved Lexi, but sometimes I had to cut her off. Otherwise she would want to text for hours.

As I was putting my phone back in my bag, it

dinged with an e-mail. When I saw who it was from, my eyes got so wide they felt like they were being overstretched.

To: Avery Lynn
From: Matt Thompson

Matt Thompson, aka my dad. Dad wasn't a good e-mailer. Well, maybe he was, but he wasn't when it came to me. The few times I had written him on non-holidays just to say hi and tell him what was going on in my life, it had taken him an entire week to get back to me. After that I stopped trying. Since Christmas wasn't for another five months, and my birthday wasn't for another seven, the fact that he was writing to me was very weird.

I clicked it open.

Dear Avery,

I know it's been a while since I've been in touch. Sorry about that—but there has been a lot going on in my life. I have some great news—I'm moving to Connecticut for a new sales job, which means that we'll be able to see each other a lot more often. I'll only be a half hour away. And even better news—I'm getting married. Her name is Lana and she has three daughters of her own. You're all very close in age (14, 12, and 8), so you'll have a lot in common.

I know this is a lot to take in, and I really hope we can get together and talk about it. I'll be in town starting this weekend, and if you're free next Sunday, I thought we could get together for brunch then.

Dad

After I finished reading it, I plopped down onto a blue slipcovered couch.

"Sweetheart? What's wrong?" my mom asked worriedly. "You're as pale as a ghost."

Which, for someone who had olive skin like I did,

didn't happen often. "It's Dad," I said, dazed. "He's . . . getting married."

My mother sighed and joined me on the couch. "He was supposed to *call* you and tell you," she said under her breath as she put her arm around me.

I whipped my head toward her. "Wait—you *knew* about this?" I asked, stunned.

She looked as guilty as the time I found her at the kitchen table eating my Halloween candy. She took a deep breath. "Yes. Yes, I did."

As she reached out to stroke my hair, I leaned back. I couldn't believe she had known about this and hadn't told me!

"He called me a week ago and let me know."

"You've known about this for a *week*?!" I squeaked.

"Yes," she admitted. "And while I can understand why you're upset that I didn't tell you, it really wasn't my news to tell—"

"I know you're great at keeping secrets, but you're not supposed to keep them from *me*!" That was another thing we didn't have in common. I was awful at keeping secrets. Especially when it came to birthday gifts.

I always ended up telling the person what I got them beforehand.

"Sweetheart, I can understand why this news is upsetting—"

"I didn't say I was upset by it," I said stubbornly as I fiddled with one of the straps of my overalls. Was I upset? I didn't even know. It wasn't like I even had any memories of my mom and dad ever being together, so who cared if he married someone else?

"Especially the idea of having three new step-sisters," she went on.

At that, I could feel tears begin to sprout from my eyes. If I am going to be honest, that part hurt a lot. I mean, my dad couldn't have been bothered with me for ten years, but now he was going to live in a house with three girls he wasn't even related to?

"But I think you should give your dad a chance," she said. This time when she went to stroke my hair, I let her. "People *can* change, you know."

"He wants me to go to brunch with him," I said, wiping my eyes.

"Good. Hopefully, they'll have pancakes wherever

you go," she replied. "You know you do your best thinking over pancakes."

I managed a smile. Mom always knew how to make me feel better.

"Only if there's real maple syrup," I replied.

"Well, of course. Who could possibly eat pancakes with fake maple syrup?" she said as she drew me close and kissed the top of my head.

I might not have had much of a dad, but I had an awesome mom.

Two

The fact that the week leading up to brunch
went so slowly meant I had lots of time to obsess
about the new family I was about to get. Mom got
so annoyed with my questions about what I thought
Lana and her daughters would be like, and how
much time she thought I'd be spending with Dad
now that he'd be living nearby, and whether I'd like
Lana's daughters, that she gave me five dollars on
Wednesday afternoon and dropped me and Lexi off
downtown a few hours before Painting Pals just so
I'd stop bothering her.

"Wow. Do you think if *I* started annoying my mom,

she'd give me money too?" Lexi asked as we walked up Main Street toward Javalicious to get Frappuccinos. They were actually called Chillsies there because Frappuccinos were a Starbucks thing, and Javalicious, along with every other business in town, was independent and got all bent out of shape if they heard you talking about chain stores. Mom said we were lucky to live in a town that wasn't "overrun by corporate greed." For the most part, downtown was a great collection of funky stores and restaurants—not to mention that a lot of them let you bring your dog inside—but I did love a good mall. Especially one that had a Forever 21.

"I don't know. Maybe," I replied. I didn't mention the fact that sometimes when Lexi was going on about her latest theory about why she and Dylan from her favorite band, All the Right Moves, were soul mates even if he didn't know it yet because he was super famous and busy jetting all around the world and dating Disney sitcom stars, her mom would rub the side of her temple like she had a really bad headache, which was probably a good indication that she was already annoyed.

As usual, Javalicious was crowded. Because it was

summer, it wasn't as packed with students from the college where Mom was an English professor, but most tables were taken up with people on their laptops or reading one of the many different newspapers and magazines that were in the basket near the front door.

"Two caramel Chillsies with shots of vanilla coming up," the owner, Chantal, said with a smile when it was my turn to order.

"Thanks, Chantal." I smiled back. That was one of the nice things about living in a small town: People remembered your order, especially if you were the kind of person who had the same thing over and over like I did. (Hello, tuna fish with Muenster cheese on wheat every day for school.) The baristas at the Starbucks in the mall never remembered my drink order. Not only that, but somehow the name on my cup would read something like "Charles" instead of "Avery."

"Any big plans this afternoon?" Chantal asked as she put the drinks in front of us.

"Not really—" I started to say.

"We're going to Painting Pals," Lexi interrupted, "but before that we're going to see if we can find Avery a new outfit for her to wear on Sunday when she has brunch with her *dad*."

Leave it to Lexi to blurt out my business to anyone who spoke English. Actually, she was an equal opportunity blurter, because she once spent, like, five minutes telling a German tourist at the Museum of Modern Art when we were on a field trip about how her mom liked to rescue animals, before realizing the woman barely spoke English. Even then she didn't stop—she just spoke louder, as if that was going to make the woman understand her better.

"Lexi," I hissed. "Stop!" I wasn't big on people knowing my business. I was the only one of my friends who didn't have a Twitter account. And the only pictures I posted on Instagram were of my jewelry or of Tabitha, my cat.

"That's cool," Chantal said. "Hope you find something," she added as she turned to walk away.

"He's getting *married*," Lexi went on, lowering her voice to a whisper when it came to "married," as if it was a bad word. "And she's going to have *three step-sisters*."

Love You Like a Sister

So much for my business staying my business, I thought as I felt my stomach tighten. While it had been semi-easy to convince myself since getting my dad's e-mail that all of this wasn't *that* big of a deal (*People get married all the time! I know tons of people with stepbrothers and stepsisters!* I had been saying to myself every night before I went to sleep), hearing it said out loud by another person was a whole other thing. It made it so . . . *real*.

Chantal's left eyebrow went up. "Wow. That's a lot to deal with."

The tightening moved into a full-blown clenching.

"Not really," I said nervously as I shoved the five-dollar bill my mom had given me across the counter. "I mean, it could be a lot worse. He could be marrying someone with, like, ten kids. Like on those reality shows."

"But they're girls," Lexi replied before I could even open my mouth. *"All girls."*

Chantal's other eyebrow went up. "True. Good luck with that."

"Why do I need luck?" I asked, my mouth all dry.

She shrugged. "I don't know. It's just that, you

♥ 21 ♥

know, girls are *tough*," she replied. "I had four sisters. My dad said that the sound track of our entire adolescence was slamming doors and crying."

"Oh, they're not like that," I said quickly.

Lexi looked at me. "How do you know? You haven't even met them yet. And you weren't even able to Instastalk them, because their accounts are private."

I didn't really know how they were going to be, of course. It was just wishful thinking. "Because if they are like that, this is going to be a mess," I said glumly.

Chantal reached across the counter and patted me on the hand. "I'm sure it'll be fine." She went into the bakery case and pulled out a raspberry hamantasch cookie and handed it to me. "Here—have this. I find that baked goods always help me in a crisis."

At least I had my subject for my "How I Spent My Summer" essay when school started back up: "How I Made It Through a Crisis," by Avery Johnson.

"How many evil stepsisters were there in *Cinderella* again?" Lexi asked later at Painting Pals as she picked out colors for our rhinear, while I sketched his horn. Because our dorse had gone over so well, we decided to do another animal combination. We thought about going with a pox (a pig/fox combination) or a cheetaroo (cheetah meets kangaroo) but settled on the rhinear, which was a combination of a bear and a rhinoceros.

"Two," I replied as I erased what I had just done. One look at my bedroom would make a person think that I wasn't much for order and organization (and they'd be right), but when it came to drawing, I would start over as many times as I needed to until I got it right. Mom said she wished I was more like that when it came to math. "Why?" I asked Lexi.

"Oh, good," Lexi said, relieved. "Maybe that means you won't have the same kind of experience she did, then."

I stopped erasing and looked at her. "Can we please stop talking about this whole thing with my dad?"

"Okay, okay. Sorry," she said, jumping around on one foot. If Lexi wasn't my best friend, she'd be really tiring to be friends with. She was always in motion. "We'll talk about something else."

"Great," I said as I picked up my pencil and started sketching again. After a moment I started to relax. Two One Two—the name of the gallery—had this way of doing that to me. I think it was because other than the art on the walls, the place was just . . . blank. Concrete floors, white walls, big metal benches. Mom said it was an "industrial" look. I thought maybe it was because Pixie, the owner, didn't have a lot of money to decorate. The art was what people called "modern," which meant sometimes you wouldn't know it was art unless it was hanging on the wall and had a sign next to it with a title. Like, say, the black Hefty garbage bag with teeth marks that the artist had titled *O'Neill Decides to Snack*. (According to Pixie, O'Neill was the artist's cat.)

Pixie walked over to look at our progress. "Great work, guys," she said with a thumbs-up as she kept moving. Pixie was always moving. Mom said that was because she had lived in Manhattan for too long and it had screwed up her nervous system. She had moved to town from there a year earlier and decided to start Painting Pals so that kids would have an opportunity to be around art while they worked on their own. Unfortunately, it hadn't really caught on. Lexi and I were the only people there that day. Usually there were at least six of us.

Lexi and I were quiet for a bit. The kind of quiet you could only be with your best friend, where it didn't feel awkward and you weren't racking your brain for something to talk about just to fill the silence. "So what are you going to wear on Sunday when you see him?" she finally asked.

I put down my pencil and stared at her. The kind of stare you could only get away with giving your best friend. One that said, *If you open your mouth one more time, I'm going to kill you.*

"Honey, it's just brunch," my mom yelled up to me on Sunday morning as I tried on yet another outfit. "Not your prom."

"I'm almost done," I yelled back. I searched through my closet for my yellow cotton cardigan to throw over the lilac striped dress I was wearing. We did a lot of yelling in our house. Not the angry kind—the kind that two people who were too lazy to walk up and down stairs did.

I couldn't find that cardigan, but I did find a peach one. Except when I put it on, not only did I not like the combination, but I no longer liked the dress, which meant it quickly joined the five other dresses that were lying in a heap on the foot of my bed.

When I heard Mom's footsteps coming up the stairs, I knew I was pushing it. I could tell from the way she was jogging up them that she had already had both of her morning coffees *plus* an espresso shot, and that her hyperness would result in more annoyance than usual, so I quickly grabbed the first dress I had tried on—a blue-and-white seersucker sheath that I had found at a garage sale last year—and put it back on.

"Okay, okay, I'm ready," I said as she stood in my doorway. "I just need to find a necklace." I walked over to my jewelry box. It was actually a tackle box, for fishing. It wasn't cute or anything, but as my grandfather had said when he gave it to me two birthdays before, "You won't find a more functional place to keep your jewels this side of Texas," whatever that meant.

I grabbed the first thing my h... carnelian flower on a black velvet cord on: a red really go with the dress, but that was kind of ...dn't putting together things that didn't go together. So... times there were epic fails, but for the most part it worked. If only that people remembered me as the girl who had a very unique style.

"Okay. Now I'm really ready," I said after I fastened the choker on my neck. I turned to Mom. "Do I look okay?"

She smiled so wide that I could see her dimples. "You look beautiful."

"Really?" I asked anxiously.

"Really," she replied as she pushed me toward the door so I wouldn't have a chance to change my mind (and my outfit) again. "I know you're nervous, but there's no reason to be."

"I'm not nervous," I lied.

She gave me the Look. The one that said, *Don't even think about lying to me because I'm your mother and I have you all figured out and always will.*

"Fine. Maybe I'm a little bit nervous," I admitted.

long bangs out of my face.

She pushed to be. I know in the past you and

"There's no't spent that much time together, but

your be different now."

course they would. My life was about to become

Cinderella's times a third stepsister.

"From my conversation with him, it sounds like he's really changed."

I sure hoped so. Otherwise this was going to be Awkward with a capital *A*.

Brunch wasn't Awkward with a capital *A*.

Not one bit.

It was AWKWARD WITH ALL CAPS.

For once, not only were we not late getting some-where—we were early. Ten minutes early, in fact.

In an e-mail he sent me on Thursday, Dad had told me to pick a place for brunch that I liked. I chose La Maison des Crêpes, which was French for House of Crepes (it said so right on the menu), but they had a lot of things other than crepes. Like regular pancakes, and omelets, and the best hot chocolate on the planet.

As usual, the parking lot was packed, but just as we were pulling in, someone was pulling out right near the entrance. Unlike Lexi, I'm not one of those people who look at everything as a sign, but in this case I took the empty space as one that brunch wouldn't be horrible. Or at least that there'd be only, like, two minutes of awkward silence as opposed to ten.

"You ready?" Mom asked as she swiped some lipstick across her mouth.

"What are you doing?"

She turned to me. "What do you mean?" she asked, and mashed her lips together.

"You never wear lipstick." She barely wore makeup, period. She looked at it like I did about the whole pajamas issue, but opposite: Why put it on when you were only going to take it off later?

She shrugged. "Yeah, well, I just felt like it today. End of story."

"End of story" was code for *We're not going to talk about this anymore, Avery, and if you push me on it, I'm going to get really annoyed.*

I knew there was no way my parents were ever

going to get back together (I had given up on that idea when I was five), but maybe she just wanted to look extra good to impress my dad. Like I did. That wasn't such a bad thing.

"He's probably not even here yet," I said as we got out of the car and walked toward the entrance. "He's usually on the late side. You know, like you. I wonder how I got to be on the early side when you're both like that," I babbled. I also wondered how I'd gotten to be such a babbler. Neither of them had that problem.

"Well, even if he's not here, we can give your name to the hostess so you won't have to wait as long for a table," she replied as we went inside.

I scanned the room. I was right—he wasn't here yet. "I'm going to go to the bathroom."

"Okay. I'll be right here," Mom said.

When I got to the ladies' room, two blond girls— one who looked to be my age; the other, a little older— were in front of the mirror over the sinks, fixing their hair. From their similar cornflower-blue eyes I assumed they were sisters. I waited for the older-looking one to slide over a bit so I could have some room, but she didn't budge, so I was forced to stand at the very corner of the vanity, which meant it poked me in the stomach if I tried to lean over and look in the mirror.

"Did you look at the menu for this place?" she asked the other one as she painted her lips with thick pink gloss. "There's not one healthy thing on the whole menu. It's all carbs."

The younger one finished braiding a small section of her hair and fastened it with a ponytail holder, before using a bobby pin to pin it back. "Ew," she said. "Gross."

"Actually, they have an egg white omelet," I chimed in as I opened my purse to take out my strawberry ChapStick. "My mom gets it when she's dieting. She says it's really good."

They looked at me, confused, like I had just said something in Russian. "Um, okay," said the older one. "Thanks."

I felt my face turn red. That wasn't a "Thanks" thanks. It was more of a "Why is this strange person talking to me?" thanks. "You're welcome," I mumbled as I uncapped my ChapStick. So much for trying to be friendly.

"And did you see how everyone is dressed around here?" she went on to her sister. "Can you say 'clearance rack 2012'?"

I glanced down at my dress. I wondered what she would think if I told her I had gotten it at a yard sale. I was tempted to, just to see the look on her face.

A toilet flushed and out of one of the stalls came another blond girl. She looked to be about eight or so, but unlike her sisters, who had obviously taken time with their outfits and accessories, she was wearing a pair of jeans and a plain pink T-shirt with what looked like chocolate smudges near the shoulder. "What's a clearance rack?" she asked.

The two older ones rolled their eyes at each other. "Where you get your clothes," the middle one replied.

Obviously used to being treated like this, the younger one just shrugged as she began to wash her hands.

The older one glanced over at me. "Is that a *ChapStick*?"

I stopped midswipe and nodded.

"I didn't know they even *made* those anymore."

My eyes narrowed. I knew an insult even if it wasn't a straight-ahead one. In fact, the ones that weren't straight ahead were even worse. "Yeah, well, I happen to like old school," I said. "Like my dress. It's vintage."

She wrinkled her nose. "I hope you washed it first."

"I like your dress," said the youngest one as she scrubbed some soap on her chocolate stain, making it even worse.

I smiled at her gratefully. "Thanks."

The older one gave her already-perfect hair one last smoothing out and sighed. "I guess we should go back out there and get this over with."

"Yeah," agreed the middle one, smoothing her own hair, but messing it up a bit in the process.

I swear as they walked out, it looked like their noses were literally stuck up. Well, the older two. The younger one had her head down because she was still scrubbing at her stain and therefore bumped into the door.

After the door had closed behind them, I let out my breath. I dug my phone out of my bag.

just had a run-in with a gaggle of BBs, I texted Lexi.

OMGOMGOMG!! BLOND OR BRUNETTE???? AND WHERE????? she texted back immediately.

blond. in the bathroom here at the restaurant. "BBs" was short for either "Blond Barbies" or "Brunette Barbies," and was a term we used for various mean girls we came across. I guess if we had ever seen any redheaded ones, then they'd have been RBs, but we never had. Maybe redheads were nicer overall.

UGH!!! I HOPE THAT'S NOT A SIGN THAT THE REST OF THE DAY IS GOING TO BE BAD.

I hadn't even thought of that. Okay, texting with Lexi was *not* helping.

gotta go. more later, I wrote, before giving myself one more once-over, picking up my bag, and going back out. When I returned to the dining room, the BBs had joined their mother at a table and looked just as bored as they had sounded in the bathroom. I hoped we wouldn't have to sit near them, because having to look at them would ruin my meal.

"Some table looks like they woke up on the wrong side of the bed this morning," Mom said as we watched the oldest girl roll her eyes at her mother, who was also blond, and also pretty. The girl was a good eye roller. The kind who could roll them really slow, making you feel even dumber. Mom turned to me. "I'm so glad you're not an eye roller."

I tried to do it, just to show her it was possible. "Ouch," I said about a quarter of a roll in. "I think they're stuck."

Mom laughed.

Just then I saw my dad walk out of the restroom. As he started coming toward me, a big smile came over his face. Wow. Mom was right—he *had* changed. Usually when he saw me, his smile was more like a flash of lightning, gone as quickly as it appeared. I didn't realize until that moment, as I smiled back, how much I had missed him. Most of the time I tried to pretend it wasn't a big deal that he lived three thousand miles away and we rarely saw each other, but it *was* a big deal. And I was really glad that was about to change.

"Hi, Dad!" I cried as I started to make my way over to him.

His smile remained, but in that moment, as he kept walking, I realized that it wasn't meant for me.

It was for the table of BBs.

Aka my soon-to-be stepsisters.

Three

♬

"Avery! Hi," my dad said as he jumped up from the table and gave me a hug, after I had gotten my legs to work and made my way over to the table. He gave me a big smile, but it still looked fake. "I can't believe how grown up you look!"

Was he completely clueless about the fact that he had forgotten to mention that brunch was going to be a party?

He turned to Mom. "What happened?"

As I blushed, Mom laughed. "Apparently, they grow up."

He gave her a hug too. "You look terrific, Monica."

She smiled. "Thanks. So do you."

By this time the blond woman had gotten up and was now hovering behind my dad, looking a little nervous. Now that she was closer, I could see that while she was pretty, she wasn't, like, *model* pretty. And she had a pimple to the left of her chin. Something about that made me feel better.

My dad took the woman's hand and pulled her forward. "Avery, Monica—this is Lana. My fiancée."

"Hi," Lana said nervously, putting out her hand for me to shake. She had pretty hands. And her nail polish was this neat blue/purple color. It was very unstepmotherish, which I liked. "It's so great to meet you, Avery. I've heard so much about you."

I shook her hand, which was damp. She might have been more nervous than I was. "It's great to meet you, too," I replied as I glanced at her daughters out of the corner of my eye. The youngest one was staring straight at me, not even trying to hide her interest. The other two were on their phones.

Lana let go of my hand and turned to Mom. "Hi. Matt speaks so highly of you."

Mom blushed. "Well, that's very nice to hear."

It *was* nice to hear. My dad got extra points for that. Which I had a feeling he'd need to use once we got to the soon-to-be-stepsisters part.

"And these are my girls," Lana said. She pointed to the youngest one. "This is Samantha—she goes by Sammi—"

"Not *all* the time," Samantha/Sammi replied. "Just sometimes."

"Right. Just sometimes," Lana corrected. "And next to her is Kayley," she went on, pointing to the middle one. "She's twelve, like you—in fact, you're just a month apart!" The way she said it made it sound like that meant we should be best friends or something.

"Neat," I replied.

Kayley, on the other hand, did not look like it was all that neat. Kayley looked like her mom was nuts for thinking it was all that exciting.

"And that one," she said, pointing at the oldest one, "is Cassie. She's fourteen."

I waited for Cassie to look up from her phone, but it wasn't happening. "Hi," I finally said.

"Hey," she said, her head still down.

Lana looked embarrassed. "She's just . . . fourteen, I guess," she laughed nervously, before turning toward her and glaring. "Cassie. Put that away," she hissed.

With a sigh Cassie put her phone in her bag and tried to look somewhat interested in what was going on, but failed.

I gave Mom the look I usually reserved for when the dentist said, "This isn't going to hurt but a bit."

She put her arm around me. "I don't think Avery was aware that this was going to be a group thing."

"Did I not mention that in the e-mail?" my dad replied, surprised. "I just thought it would be a more economical use of our time to do it all at once."

"No, I don't think you did mention it," she replied.

He looked at me. "Sorry about that. I guess I was just so excited for you to meet everyone."

At least one of us was. I shrugged. "Whatever."

Even without looking at her, I knew that my mom was probably giving me a *Don't "whatever" me* look. She hated that word. She said it was way too teenagery for her liking, and she had one more year to tell me not to use it.

"Okay, then. I guess I should get going so you guys can eat." She turned to me. "Have fun," she said, pushing my bangs out of my eyes.

I pushed them back in. *Yeah right*, my eyes said, even though "Sure" was what came out of my mouth.

"We'll drop her off after we eat," my dad said.

"Great. See you then," she replied as she walked away.

"I'll have the blueberry pancakes and an orange juice, please," I said when the waitress asked for my order.

"Small or large?" she asked.

"Large, please," I replied.

Cassie's eyebrow shot up.

"What?" I asked.

She shrugged. "Nothing. I'm just not used to seeing someone order so much food," she replied. "Things are just different in California, I guess."

Before I could say anything, the waitress asked for her order. "I'll have the egg white omelet, please," she said. "No toast. No hash browns."

From the look on her face, the waitress was as surprised as I was that someone would willingly order something so boring. "Extra fruit?" she asked.

"No, thank you," Cassie said.

"Juice?"

"Just water, please."

Now it was the waitress's turn to raise an eyebrow. "Okay, then. I'll put that right in," she said as she walked away.

Cassie and I flashed each other a fake smile.

This was going to be a long brunch.

Over the next hour and ten minutes, this was what I learned:

1. Girls from California didn't use butter.
2. Girls from California didn't have much interest in hearing about the hobbies of girls from New York.
3. My father smiled a lot more now that he was with Lana.

4. And he smiled a lot at her girls.
5. Which made me kind of jealous.

"I was so looking forward to this," he said, patting me on the arm while I finished my last bite of pancake. I wasn't even hungry anymore—I did it just to make Cassie squirm.

Maybe I would have been too. If, you know, I had known it was going to happen.

Lana and the girls were busy talking about where to go shopping to decorate their new house. It wasn't surprising that garage sales didn't come up.

"Isn't Lana great?" he asked with a smile.

"Yeah," I agreed. That wasn't a lie—she was actually very nice. She had made a point all through brunch to ask me lots of questions about my life and seemed genuinely interested in the answers. Unlike her daughters. Well, two of her daughters—Sammi kind of paid attention. That is, when she wasn't busy spilling food on herself and scrubbing the stains, often making them worse.

"And I just knew you and the girls would hit it off."

I looked over at him to see if he was joking. He wasn't.

The waitress brought the check over. After he gave her his credit card, he turned to me. "Before we leave, Lana has something she wants to ask you."

It probably wasn't where I got my clothes. With her completely unwrinkled red-striped sundress (I had never seen my mother iron; I wasn't even sure we owned one), she looked like she had stepped out of a magazine.

Lana took my dad's hand. "I was wondering if you'd be one of my bridesmaids," she said shyly.

What?! Being asked to be a bridesmaid was a huge deal. And I had known her for only an hour and ten minutes. "Oh. Wow. I've never been a bridesmaid before," I replied.

Cassie gave a quick eye roll. She was great at a fast eye roll too—I had to give her that. It was so quick that you couldn't even really call her on it. It was too bad we'd probably never be friends, because I would have loved for her to teach me.

"So you'll do it?" Lana asked.

"Sure. I'd love to." Okay, "love" was stretching it a bit, but what else were you supposed to say when someone asked you to be a bridesmaid in her wedding? Especially when that person looked so hopeful.

"Great! That's wonderful!" my dad said, pulling me toward him and giving me a side hug. I couldn't remember seeing him this excited . . . ever. It was a nice feeling—the idea that I could make him happy like this.

Maybe my mother was right—maybe things *would* be different now.

For the first time since I sat down at the table, I felt good.

Until I looked across and saw three faces staring back at me. Three faces that, unlike their mother's, did not look excited about my answer.

They had come in two cars so that, according to my dad, he and I could have some "alone time" on the fifteen-minute drive back to my house. Usually when we were in the car, there was a lot of uncomfortable silence. To the point where I'd turn on the radio and start fiddling with it, and because I wasn't sure what kind of music he liked because I spent so little time with him, I'd keep switching stations in hopes that he'd finally say, "Go back—I really like that song." But instead what he usually ended up saying was "Avery, please just settle on one station, okay? I'm getting a headache." Which would make me feel worse and result in all sorts of babbling about whatever song was playing on whatever station I settled on. But this time there wasn't silence. In fact, my dad was so talkative that I felt like if he didn't stop, *I'd* be the one with the headache. He told me all about the house they had bought ("At first I thought it would be nice for you and Sammi to share a room, because I know how much I enjoyed sharing a room with my brother when I was growing up, even if I didn't like it at the time, but Lana said there'd be no reason for it, seeing that the house has five bedrooms"). And how he and Lana had met ("One of the guys I work with finally convinced me to sign up for one of those online dating sites, and when I read her profile and she mentioned she was a huge basketball fan, I was already in love"). And how he had proposed ("I had planned this whole romantic weekend in Santa Cruz, but I was so nervous that I ended up asking her while we were in line at Starbucks").

He even looked different than the last time I had seen him. The circles were gone from under his eyes, and his shoulders weren't hunched up near his ears, and his mouth seemed to be stuck in a permanent smile. He looked happy, which, I realized as he hummed along with the radio, was something I hadn't seen much of before.

Usually when he pulled up in front of my house, he was in such a hurry to get going that he left the engine running as we said good-bye. But this time he turned it off.

"What are you doing?" I asked, confused.

"Just spending some time with my daughter," he said with a smile. "Is that okay?"

"Sure," I said as I smiled back, hoping it looked genuine. Which is hard to do when you're really confused because your dad has been body-snatched and replaced with some happy, chatty guy.

"Aren't Lana's girls great?"

I could feel my smile flicker. "Uh-huh."

"I like that they're from California," he went on. "Not like it's a different country or anything, but I like that they'll be able to share their experience with you."

"Yeah. That'll be cool."

"Sammi's a riot," he laughed. "Always spilling stuff on herself. Did you notice that?"

"I did."

"And Kayley is *very* smart. She got all As on her report card last year."

"So did I," I shot back. Well, all A minuses. Which was kind of the same.

"You did?" he said, surprised. "I had no idea."

Maybe you would have if you read my e-mails, I wanted to say. I knew I had mentioned it in one of them.

"That's really great, Avery. I'm very proud of you."

I kind of hated how I could go from being so mad at him to being happy that I had made him happy. "Thanks. When school starts this year, I think—"

"And Cassie is a real force of nature. She was president of her class last year. *And* captain of the lacrosse team."

"Well, I started an art club at school last year," I said. "We have only ten members right now, but I bet it's going to grow this year. And I sold three pieces of jewelry last month without even planning to. People saw it on me and said they liked it, and when I said I'd made it, they said they wished they could buy something just like that, and I sold it to them on the spot."

"Wow. That's very impressive." But the look on his face made it seem like the lacrosse team was more impressive.

"Thanks." I took out my phone. "Do you want to see some pictures?"

"I'm glad you're going to have an older sister," he continued. "It's nice to have someone to look up to."

I put down my phone. This was *not* cool. It was like all he wanted to do was sit there and brag to me about these girls who weren't even related to him, and everything that his *real* daughter had done came up short!

"I think you'll learn a lot from her."

Like what? How to make people feel small and stupid?

He squeezed my hand. "I'm so glad we had this talk," he said as he started to open his door.

If what he meant was him going on and on about how great Lana's girls were and totally ignoring everything I said, then, sure, I guess it was a talk.

"This is going to be great," he said with a smile.

Really? In what universe?

FOUR

"Maybe they were just nervous," Mom said as
we poked around the bead store later that day. "People
show their nervousness in different ways." When I told
her how brunch had gone, and about the conversation
with my dad, she had suggested we take a field trip
to the store and then get ice cream. And she'd let me
invite Lexi.

"That's true," Lexi agreed from the floor, where
she was picking up a box of silver beads that she had
knocked over. Lexi was a bit on the klutzy side. "Take me,
for example: When I get nervous, I knock things over."

"Are you nervous now?" Mom asked.

"No. This was just a miscellaneous knockover," she replied.

Mom laughed. "You're one of a kind, Lexi."

"That's what my mom says too."

I fingered the tiger beads I was thinking of buying. They would look great with this black butterfly I had found at a thrift store when we visited my grandparents while they were in Florida a few months back. "Or maybe they were just stuck up," I said.

"Or maybe they were just stuck up," Mom agreed. "But even if that's the case, you might have to be the bigger person and just keep being extra nice even when it's the last thing you want to do."

The "bigger person" thing. That was a favorite saying of Mom's. I felt like I was always being asked to do it. I sighed. "Why do I always have to be the bigger person?"

"You're really good at it, you know," Lexi pointed out. "Remember fourth-grade science class, with that weird kid Jimmy Pagano? The one who used to glue his fingers together on purpose? And he kept kicking your chair, and Mrs. Olson told you to be the bigger person and move because he obviously had issues and wasn't going to stop?"

"Yeah. And he smelled like bologna that had been left in a hot car for hours." I shuddered.

Lexi wrinkled her nose. "Right. I forgot that part. Ew."

"Sweetie, they're going to be your family," Mom said. "That's why."

"Well, maybe I won't have to do much for the wedding," I said.

"You're a bridesmaid," she replied. "That's a big honor. And a lot of responsibility."

"Well, maybe it's the kind of wedding where I'll just have to show up, like, the day of the wedding," I said hopefully. "And everything else can be done, like, online."

Just as I said that, my phone beeped with a text.

Hey Avery! It's Lana. I was wondering if you were free on Tuesday afternoon to get together to talk about the wedding. We've got a lot to do in the next month! xo Lana

Or maybe not.

Lana texted me that Monday to ask if I wouldn't mind coming over to their new house the next day because she had to wait around for the cable guy to come install their cable.

okay, I texted back.

Wonderful! Thank you so much! was her response. I so appreciate it!

"Lana's really big on exclamation points," I told Mom as we drove over there on Tuesday. I couldn't help but notice that she had changed out of her cut-off jean shorts and tank top into one of her nicer sundresses. Not that I was one to talk—I had tried on four outfits before I finally settled on a denim miniskirt and a lilac gauze shirt with bell sleeves.

"Is that such a bad thing? Maybe she's really excited about getting to know you."

I shrugged. "Maybe. But I thought you didn't like overexclamators."

"I never said I didn't *like* them. I said . . . they were awfully loud on the page," she replied.

We smiled at each other. And then mine faded.

"What's the matter?" Mom asked.

"I was just thinking about Cassie," I replied. "I took

your advice. You know, about sending her a friend request on Facebook? She wouldn't even accept it!"

"I find that hard to believe," Mom said. "She probably just hasn't seen it yet."

"She *deleted* it."

I knew my mom well enough to catch the *Oh boy, that's not good* look that flashed across her face. "Well, maybe she's more of an Instagram person."

That was my mom—definitely a (coffee) cup-half-full person. She grabbed my hand. "Honey—we talked about this. She's probably having her own feelings about the wedding. People deal with their anxiety in lots of different ways. But as long as you continue—"

"Are you going to say 'to be the bigger person'?" I interrupted.

"Yes."

As we turned onto my dad's street, I sighed. "Yeah, well, if I get any bigger, I'm not going to fit through the car door."

"Wow. This is . . . wow," Mom murmured as we

drove through the development, each house bigger than the next. Unlike our neighborhood, which was full of funky little cottages that were painted different colors and had, as Mom liked to say, "a lot of history that they like to show off" (code for they were old and the owners didn't have the money to fix them up because most of the people who lived in the neighborhood were artists or professors), this neighborhood had perfect houses. Perfectly cut lawns. Perfect flower beds. Perfect cars in the driveways that didn't have any dings and looked to have been washed that morning. The houses also all looked exactly alike. So much so that if you were coming home after work and it was dark, it would be easy enough to pull into the wrong driveway.

A few houses later Beatrice (that was the name we'd given the GPS lady) announced we were at our destination, and I saw Lana's shiny black SUV in the driveway. As we pulled up, the front door opened and she came bounding out, also in a sundress. Hers, unlike Mom's, looked like it had been ironed.

When we got out of the car, Lana gave me a hug.

"Hey, Avery. It's great to see you again!" She had a really nice smile. A very white one.

"You, too," I replied. She smelled good. Perfumy, but not the sickly sweet kind that made me gag.

She walked over to Mom. "And you, too, Monica!"

Before Mom could reply, Lana pulled her in for a hug.

"Oh. Wow. Look at that. We're hugging," Mom said, a little surprised. "That's so nice."

"Would you like to come in for something to drink?" Lana asked.

"I'd love to, but I'm off to yoga."

"So you're a yogi!" Lana exclaimed. "I had no idea."

"Yeah. I've been practicing for a while." Mom was trying to sound casual about it, but I knew she was proud of the fact that she had been going for five years. And I was proud of *her*. She wasn't great at committing to things, especially exercise-related things.

"Oh yeah? Me too. How long have you been practicing?"

"About five years."

"That's great," Lana said as she flashed another smile.

"What about you?" Mom asked.

"Oh, I don't know . . . I think . . . fifteen?" She wasn't all puffed up about it. It was almost like she sounded a little embarrassed.

Mom's face fell like the chocolate soufflé we had tried to make for Thanksgiving last year. "Wow. That's terrific. Very impressive." She turned to me. "Isn't that impressive, Avery?"

"Totally," I agreed.

"Do you do yoga, Avery?" Lana asked.

I shook my head. "Nope. The one time I tried, I slipped and broke my toe."

"Ouch. That's too bad. Let me guess: You're a tennis player. Like your dad."

My dad played tennis? That was news to me. I shook my head again. "No. Last time I played, I hit myself in the head with the racquet and got a black eye."

She laughed. "You're funny." She stopped when she saw that Mom and I weren't joining her. "Oh. You're serious?"

I nodded. "I'm not all that coordinated."

"She gets that from my side of the family," Mom said proudly.

Lana looked like she didn't know whether she was joking or not. (She wasn't.)

Mom turned to me. "Okay, then. I'm going to go. What time should I pick you up?"

"Oh, don't worry about that. I'll drop her off."

"There's no need for that," Mom said.

"No, really—it's not a big deal. Plus I need to learn the area."

Mom shrugged. "Okay. Great. Thanks."

I knew her well enough to know that she was trying to figure out what she should clean first before we got there and Lana invited herself in.

She leaned over and kissed me. "I'll see you later. Have fun."

"I will," I lied.

As I watched her walk away, I felt like I did the first day of sleepaway camp when I was ten. Already homesick. When I turned back to Lana, she was smiling again. I wondered if it hurt to do it so much.

"Ready to go in?" she asked.

I nodded.

"The girls have been so excited for you to get here," she said over her shoulder.

I was surprised about how much I liked Lana. It was too bad to find out that she was a liar.

"I've been excited too," I replied. Okay, so I was a liar as well.

When we walked in, it was hard to believe that they had lived in the house for only a week. It was perfectly put together, but in such a way that it *didn't* look put together. There was a lot of glass and sharp corners, and it looked somewhat unfriendly, sort of like a tall, thin cheerleader. There was no dust or fingerprints on any of it. Our furniture, on the other hand, had smudges on it even if we had cleaned it, like, five minutes before.

"This place is *nice*," I blurted out.

"Oh, thanks, but we're still pretty far away from having it all done," Lana said.

Jeez. I could only imagine what it would look like then.

"Come on. Let's go see the girls," she said as she turned.

I followed her to the family room, where Kayley and Cassie were sprawled out on different couches watching one of the *Real Housewives* shows, while Sammi was busy practicing headstands . . . and failing.

"Girls? Avery's here."

Sammi fell over and popped back up on her knees. "Hi," she chirped.

I smiled. She was really cute. "Hi," I replied. Maybe I'd ask her if she could teach me to do a headstand. I was not what you'd call athletic. In fact, other kids in school now came up to me for suggestions of excuses to get out of gym class.

"I'll be right back," Lana said. "I'm going to get us some snacks."

Cassie and Kayley continued to watch TV, glued to a commercial about floor wax. As I waited for Lana to come back, I looked at the framed photos that were on the built-in shelves—one way not to feel even more awkward than you already did when being ignored.

Lots of my dad and Lana, in beachlike settings or ski-
ing. A ton of the girls that followed them through the
years. Ballet. Horseback riding. Canoeing. A few of the
five of them, already looking like a family. I searched
the shelves for some of me but found only one. My
third-grade school picture, the one where the ends
of my hair were wet because I had been chewing on
them beforehand, which was a nervous habit I had for
a while. It wasn't even in a frame—it was propped up
against the corner of the shelf.

"Girls. Turn that off, please," Lana ordered as she
returned with a tray full of chips and guacamole and a
pitcher of lemonade. She might have been a smiler, but
I could tell that when she got mad, she was probably
pretty good at that as well. "Thank you," she said as
Kayley clicked the TV off.

Lana's smile was back on. "Avery. Please. Have
a seat."

Seeing that Sammi and Lana were now taking
up the two chairs, that left me with having to choose
a couch, which was almost as bad as standing in the
middle of the cafeteria on the first day of school as a

new kid. Deciding that Kayley was the safer choice, I sat down with her, as close to the far edge as possible.

"I apologize for the lack of food. I hope you like chips and guacamole. It was the fastest thing I could whip up."

"You *made* this?" I said, impressed. I was pretty sure Mom wouldn't have known where to begin making guacamole.

"Sure. You've never made it before?"

I shook my head. Our version of cooking at home was popping things in the microwave.

"Well, next time you're here, I'll teach you," she said.

Lana definitely didn't fit the evil-stepmother mold. While it was a relief, it also made me feel a little guilty, like I wasn't being loyal toward my own mother by liking her.

Lana pushed the tray toward me. "Please. Have some."

No one else had made a move to have some, so I definitely wasn't going to be the first. "Thanks, but I'm not that hungry," I lied. "I had a big breakfast." Just then my stomach decided to let out the biggest, longest, loudest gurgle in the history of gurgles. It was so loud that Cassie stopped the texting I could see her doing from behind a throw pillow.

I grabbed my stomach to try and stop it as they all looked at me. "That must be the bacon."

Everyone laughed. Well, everyone except Cassie, which wasn't a surprise. And when Kayley saw that Cassie wasn't laughing, she stopped.

"It's nice to see you have your dad's sense of humor," Lana said.

My dad was funny? Really? Maybe you had to spend a bunch of time with him for that to come out.

"Did you know they make chocolate bars with bacon in them?" Kayley said. "It sounds gross, but it's really good."

"My friend Lexi loves those," I replied. "I once tried one that had wasabi in it. You know, that spicy stuff that you mix with soy sauce for sushi? That was *really* weird."

Kayley wrinkled her nose. "That sounds gross."

"It was," I agreed. I racked my brain, trying to think of something else to keep the conversation going, but came up blank. And once Kayley caught Cassie's eye, she sank back on her side of the couch and went back to ignoring me.

"Okay, so we've got a lot to do before the wedding," Lana announced. She turned to Kayley. "Kayley, how much time do we have left?"

"Four weeks, four days"—she grabbed Lana's phone—"twenty hours and"—she glanced at it again—"thirty minutes."

Lana turned to me. "Kayley's a whiz with numbers."

She looked embarrassed. "No, I'm not."

"Maybe you can help me with my math homework sometime," I joked.

She gave me a dirty look.

"Or not," I muttered. Could I say *anything* right?

"So I'm sure you've all heard about the tradition of the bride wearing something old, something new, something borrowed, and something blue," Lana went on.

"Um, yeah," Cassie said. "Anyone who's ever watched one of those bridal shows knows about that."

I had never seen a bridal show, but even I knew about that.

"I don't need the extra commentary, Cassie," Lana warned. "Anyways, I thought it would be fun if we split the tasks up. Kayley, I thought you could be in charge of the something new; Sammi, you could find something blue—"

"I love blue," Sammi replied. "It's my favorite color!"

Lana smiled. "I know. That's why I'm asking you. I'll deal with something borrowed, because my friend Charlotte said I could borrow this pearl bracelet of hers that I've always loved. And you two," she said, looking at me and Cassie, "can be in charge of something old."

The two of us looked at each other. *Seriously?* Out of everyone, I had to be paired up with *her*? That was just cruel.

Neither of us looked excited. Which was probably the only time we'd have something in common.

I was tempted to offer just to do it myself. It would give Cassie more time to sit on the couch and watch shows about fake-looking people. And then I heard my mom's voice: *Be the bigger person.* I pasted a giant fake smile on my face. "Great!" I chirped. Ow. Fake smiling really hurt your cheeks.

"Whatever," Cassie replied.

I think it was safe to say my mom wouldn't like Cassie all that much.

I could see from Lana's eyes that she was getting more and more frustrated with her. "Wonderful. Matt and I thought this would be a great way for you girls to bond." It was obvious that in this case "girls" meant the two of us. It was comforting to know that at least my dad was aware that blending this family together wasn't going to be a piece of cake. If anything, it was going to be like cookie batter with lots of nuts and chocolate chips—really, really bumpy.

Bigger person . . . bigger person. "I'm glad we got the old part," I said. "I love vintage stuff. I know lots of places we can check out for that."

Cassie raised her eyebrow. "You mean, like, stuff from thrift stores?"

I shrugged. "Thrift stores . . . garage sales . . ."

"I don't think I've ever actually *been* to a garage sale," she replied.

Why did that not surprise me? I grabbed my leather purse and held it up. "I got this at a garage sale."

She moved back a bit, as if it was about to infect her.

This was going *really* well.

Lana got up and started toward the kitchen. "I'm going to leave you girls alone to come up with a game plan. Have fun!"

Have fun? That definitely wasn't going to happen. After sitting there in silence for a while, Kayley reading a magazine, Sammi flipping her legs over the back of the couch, and Cassie scrolling through her Instagram feed, I realized that if I didn't take charge and try to organize us, nothing was going to get done. Luckily, I was good at doing that.

"So, um, does anyone have any ideas?" I asked tentatively. "Because if no one else does, I might have a few." Okay, maybe I didn't sound all that take-charge-ish at the moment, but it was a start.

"What kind of ideas?" Kayley asked, bored, as she twirled a lock of hair around her finger.

"Well, in terms of the new thing, when I was shopping with my friend Lexi the other day, we saw these really pretty earrings," I said. "They're in the shape of roses, but tiny ones, so tiny that you almost can't tell they're roses. And what made them really cool is that they're gold, but, like, this pinkish gold—"

"Our mother doesn't have pierced ears," she cut me off. Which was probably a good thing, because who knew what would have come out of my mouth if I had kept going.

"Oh. Okay," I replied. "Well, maybe you still want to check out the store. I just remembered that we also saw this supercute little bag. It's not big—just big enough to hold some makeup and stuff like that—and it's beaded, but not, like, *bright* beads, more like—"

She finally put her magazine aside and looked at me. "She just said she's wearing a pearl bracelet. I don't know if that would look good with a beaded bag."

Way to make someone feel about two feet tall. "Okay. You might be right," I agreed, even though I personally liked to put things together that didn't necessarily seem to go together. Like rainbow tights and purple high-tops. Or popcorn and hot fudge sauce (that was mine and Lexi's favorite pig-out food). "There's also this other store I like—"

"Thanks for all the suggestions, but seeing that *I'm*

the one who's supposed to come up with the something new, I should probably just find something
myself," she cut me off, sounding annoyed.

I shrank back into the couch. "I was just trying to
help," I replied softly. "I just thought because you guys
just moved here—"

She held up her phone. "That's what Yelp is for."

"I'd like to go to that store," Sammi piped up.
"And I'll just say, 'Please show me all of your blue
stuff.'"

I smiled at her. "Okay. I'll take you. And afterward
we can go to my favorite ice cream place."

"I LOVE ice cream!" she exclaimed. She pointed
to her sisters. "They only eat frozen yogurt. I think it
tastes disgusting."

I thought it tasted disgusting too, but I didn't dare
say that. "They also have frozen yogurt. And tons of
toppings to choose from." I liked the toppings better
than the yogurt.

"How exciting," Cassie said.

I couldn't tell if she was being sarcastic or not. And
it wasn't like I was going to ask.

Lana popped her head in. "How's it going? Are you having fun?" she asked hopefully.

"Totally," Cassie said.

Lana smiled. "I thought you would. Avery, your dad called—he'll be home in about a half hour and will take you home."

"Great," I replied. It would probably be rude to pull out my phone and set the timer.

"Okay, well, I'll let you girls get back to planning," she said.

We went back to the awkward-silence thing.

"So . . . do you want to talk about the something old?" I finally asked. It was either continue with brainstorming or sit in awkward silence.

"I guess," Cassie said, bored.

"What do you think about a scrapbook?" I asked. Before I started making jewelry, I was way into scrapbooking. Not only did I take a class at the library, but Mrs. Agnelli, my art teacher, asked if I would help teach the little kids in the after-school enrichment program.

Cassie wrinkled her nose again. "A *scrapbook*? That's so . . . five years ago."

I shrugged. "I think it could be cool. People always save things that are important to them. Like ticket stubs and e-mails and pictures, and they always think they'll get around to putting them all together, but they never do," I replied. "We could get hold of all the stuff that has to do with my dad and your mom falling in love and put it together."

She shook her head. "My mom doesn't save that kind of stuff."

"She doesn't save pictures?" I asked.

"Yeah, of course *pictures*. Anyone with a phone can save those. But not ticket stubs. That's just corny."

I saved all sorts of stuff. Especially ticket stubs. I had the stub from every movie I had ever seen. I was planning on gluing them on a little side table one day when I had enough to cover it. I crossed my arms. "Fine. Do *you* have any ideas, then?"

"Not yet. But I'm sure I'll come up with something."

After their reactions, I figured I shouldn't bring up my other idea—the one I really thought would be neat—which was me making a charm bracelet for Lana made up of charms representing us four girls and my dad. I could only imagine what her response to that would be. For some reason I was embarrassed to tell them I made jewelry.

So *she* would come up with something? Not *we* would? "I thought we were supposed to do this together," I said.

"Well, yeah, but she's *our* mother, so we know what she likes. I mean, this *is* only your second time meeting her," Cassie replied.

I glared at her. I wanted to think that she had no idea of how mean that sounded, but I had a feeling I was wrong.

Five

there are no words to describe my mortification at the moment, I texted Lexi from the bathroom. I had been hiding in there for the last ten minutes or so and had spent most of that time texting her a recap of what had gone on since I had been at the house.

DO YOU WANT ME TO GET MY THESAURUS AND TRY AND HELP YOU COME UP WITH SOME? she texted back.

I sighed. It was great to have a best friend who was always there when you needed her, but sometimes what she said when trying to help was not all that helpful.

Love You Like a Sister

Right then I heard my dad walk into the house. if you need me, i'll be the one hiding under a rock, I typed, before putting my phone down.

"Where's Avery?" I heard him ask Lana after they were done kissing. (Unfortunately, because the bathroom was right off the kitchen, I could hear that as well.)

"In the living room with the girls," she replied.

"No, she's not."

"She's not?" she said, confused. "She was a half hour ago. . . ."

Good to know that if I was kidnapped, no one would notice for a few hours. I was tempted to keep hiding for a little bit but decided that would be mean.

"Oh, hi," I said, trying to look surprised as I walked out of the bathroom. I didn't want them to think I had been eavesdropping. Or, worse, listening to them kissing.

"Hey there," my dad said. At first it looked like he was going to hug me, but then he changed his mind at the last minute and just patted my shoulder. "How's it going? Have you been having fun with the girls?"

"Yeah," I lied.

"Isn't the house great?" he asked.

"I haven't really—"

"What do you think of your room? It's pretty cool, huh?"

"I don't—"

"I haven't seen your room in your mom's house, but I can't imagine it's as big as this."

Exactly. He had never seen my room because he had never bothered to come inside when he dropped me off.

"Actually, I love my room at home," I replied, accenting the word "home." "I have this iron bed that we found on Craigslist that's covered with a ton of pillows that have all sorts of neat covers, and last year Mom said we could repaint it and I chose this really pretty lilac. A soft one, because Mom said if it was too bright, it would keep me up at night, and—"

"That sounds really nice, Avery," he said, cutting me off.

I wasn't even done yet.

"But is it as big as your room here, though?" he asked.

"I wouldn't know because I haven't seen it."

He looked surprised. "Lana didn't show you your room?"

"The girls were so deep into bonding that I didn't want to break the moment," Lana said.

Bonding. Right. They were bonding to their phones, but not with me.

"Well, let's go see it, then," he said.

I followed him upstairs.

"This is Sammi's room," he announced as I peeked in. It was cute. A purple beanbag chair. A canopy bed with a rainbow comforter. Books and toys kind of organized, but not really.

We kept walking. "And this is Kayley's."

If Sammi's was fun and sweet and inviting, Kayley's was the exact opposite. It was serious and not a place where you'd want to hang out. Even the bed looked uncomfortable. Everything was navy and white, and the covers were pulled tight, and there were no messy piles on her desk, like on mine. In fact, there were no piles, period.

"It looks very . . . *neat*," I said. That was the best I could come up with.

"Yeah. Kayley is very . . . *serious* about her neatness."

No kidding.

Next to it was Cassie's room. If *Seventeen* did a photo spread of the perfect teenage girl's room, this would be it. Big TV. Closet full of clothes and shoes. Bulletin board covered with pictures of her hugging various friends, having a great time.

"And this . . . ," my dad said when we turned to the room across the hall, "is your room!"

It was big, that was for sure. And the fact that it was so big made it all that much more disappointing when I saw how it had been decorated. I didn't know what my dad had told Lana about me, but it had to have been something along the lines that I was a very frilly girl. There were ruffles everywhere: on the bed, on the curtains—even on the *towels* that were laid out neatly on the bed.

"Don't you just love it?" he asked excitedly.

"I . . . wow—look at these curtains. They're so . . . *pink*," I replied. I hadn't answered the question, but I didn't want to lie.

He smiled. "That's because I told her pink is your favorite color."

It was . . . back when I was *four*.

He looked at his watch. "We should get going. I told your mom I'd have you back by five."

When I went to say good-bye, Lana said, "If you're free on Saturday, I was thinking we could go look for your bridesmaid dresses."

Oh boy. I could only imagine what that would be like. "Sure. Sounds great." I made sure to make my smile extra big.

"Terrific. I'll text you about a time." She hugged me. "I hope you like your room." She leaned in. "We had decided on a budget for all of your rooms, but I went a little over with yours," she whispered.

I knew that was supposed to make me feel special, but it just made me feel worse. "You didn't have to do that," I said.

"I know. I just wanted to make sure you feel extra comfortable when you're here. So it'll be just as much of a home for you as your other home."

Ugh. Now I felt even *worse*.

When we got into the car, my dad started with the talking-nonstop thing again. This time it was about his new job, and the country club they had just joined, and the great schools that the girls had gotten into. Finally I couldn't take it anymore.

"Dad."

"Oh, and did I mention where we're going on our honeymoon? Italy! I can't wait—"

"*Dad,*" I said louder.

He looked over at me, surprised. I hadn't meant for it to come out so sharply.

"Sorry," I said.

"What is it, Avery?"

My face was hot. "It's just . . . do you think we could talk about something other than your life and how great the girls are?" I blurted out.

He looked embarrassed. "I didn't realize—"

Now that I had opened my mouth, I couldn't stop. "I barely see you for years, and when I do, it's all about your new family."

"I'm sorry for being so insensitive. What would you like to talk about, then?"

I shrugged. "I don't know."

We drove in silence for a bit. Which was almost as bad as hearing him go on and on about the girls.

Finally I spoke. "Do you even know what grade I'm going into?"

"Of course I do!" he said defensively. "You're going into . . . sixth."

"I'm going into *seventh*," I corrected.

He looked embarrassed. "I'm sorry."

After that I didn't say anything. I just spent the rest of the drive staring out the window.

When I told Mom at dinner (Indian food, our favorite) about my conversation with my dad, she was really proud of me.

"It takes a lot of courage to tell someone how you feel like that," she said as she put some more saag paneer on her plate. Lucky for her, I didn't like it because it had spinach in it, which meant she got to eat the whole thing. And lucky for me, she didn't like chickpeas, which meant that I could have all of the chana masala. "I'm glad you cleared the air. How do you feel?"

I ripped off a piece of naan, which is this yummy bread, and thought about it as I chewed. "I feel like . . . my stomach doesn't hurt anymore," I said after I swallowed.

Mom nodded. "Because you didn't keep your feelings inside."

I dipped some of the bread in some raita, which is a yogurt-y sauce with cucumbers in it. "But I feel like things are even more awkward now."

"Well, sometimes that's part of the process," she explained. "The important thing is that you spoke your truth. You can't go wrong with that." She reached over and pushed my bangs out of my eyes. "Sweetheart, it's going to take a while for you and your dad to establish more of a relationship. It's not going to happen overnight."

I sighed. "I know." I think he was so embarrassed about not knowing what grade I was in that when we got to my house, he didn't even ask to come inside. Which, frankly, was fine with me. "But what about Cassie and them? How do I deal with them?"

"Well, if it were me, I think I'd just keep—"

"Being the bigger person?" I interrupted before she could say it.

"Yeah."

I sighed. "I *have* been. And it's not working."

"Give it another shot on Saturday when you go dress shopping," she suggested. "I think you need to remember that they're probably just as nervous about this new family as you are."

"Somehow I have a hard time believing Cassie gets nervous."

She reached over to my plate and tore off a piece of naan. "You never know. Sometimes it's the ones who are the most put together on the outside who are the most frightened on the inside."

My something-new and something-old ideas might have been shot down by Kayley and Cassie, but as Saturday got closer, I felt more and more confident that there was no way they wouldn't be impressed when they saw my shopping skills.

My talent for finding treasures at garage sales carried over to malls as well. All the hours Lexi and I had spent there had made it so that I could walk into a store and within five minutes have at least ten items in my arms to try on, seven of which would be yeses. If I could find the perfect dress for us to wear, maybe the BBs would start treating me more like a sister and less like some stray cat that had shown up at their house that their mother was forcing them to be nice to because she was way into rescuing animals, like Lexi's mom.

Mom dropped me off at the mall a little early on Saturday so she could get to yoga on time. Actually, she dropped me off early so she could get another cup of coffee before yoga. Because yoga was supposed to relax you and coffee made you all jittery, it seemed to defeat the purpose, but when I mentioned that a while back, I got "A Look" meant *That's enough, Avery*, so I didn't bring it up again.

Because I had some time before Lana and the BBs got there, I decided to go to Starbucks and get us all drinks to keep up our energy while shopping. I put a lot of thought into ordering (much to the annoyance of the people behind me), finally settling on Caramel

Ribbon Crunch Frappuccinos. I wanted the BBs to know that I had good taste not only in clothes, but in drinks as well.

I was sitting next to the fountain with the tray of drinks a few minutes later, trying not to spill mine on my light-blue T-shirt that said "Best" (Lexi had a matching one that said "Friend"), when they walked up.

"Hey, Avery," Lana said warmly as she hugged me. She had the same perfume on as she had the other day, and it smelled just as good. Mom didn't believe in perfume—she said that she was quite happy wearing eau de life. Which, not surprisingly, smelled a lot like coffee.

Out of the corner of my eye, I saw Cassie and Kayley share an eye roll. Kind of like me and Lexi had done when Anna Mercer waved her arm wildly during history to answer every question that Mr. Mahoney asked. It wasn't my fault that Lana was being so nice to me.

Once she let go, I turned to the three of them. "Hey," I said with a big smile. I wasn't going to let them get to me. At least, that's what I had said to the mirror over and over this morning as I got dressed.

"Hi!" Sammi replied with her own smile. Until she glanced over at her sisters and saw that they were looking at me like I was a dog who had just gotten sprayed by a skunk. Then her smile dimmed.

Cassie looked me up and down. "I can see you went all out with your outfit today."

I looked down at the jean miniskirt I had paired with the T-shirt. "What's wrong with a T-shirt and miniskirt?"

She shrugged. "Nothing . . . if you're, like, hanging out in your room watching TV." They, on the other hand, *had* gone all out with their outfits. Cassie was wearing a blue-and-black-print maxidress, and Kayley was in really nice jeans and a tank top that was edged with rhinestones. Even Samantha—who was a bit of a tomboy—was in a T-shirt and flowered skirt.

I felt my face turn red as Kayley laughed. "I like to be comfortable when I shop," I replied tightly as I took in the heels that Cassie had on. "It's my favorite form of exercise."

"Oh, I agree on the comfort thing," Lana said. She pointed at her own shoes—a pair of perfectly white

Keds that looked like they didn't know what the word
"dirt" meant. "So are you ready to do some shopping,
Avery?" she asked. She sounded like a game show
host who was super hopeful that the contestants
wanted to play.

"Definitely," I replied. I pointed to Forever 21. "I
don't know where you were thinking we should start,
but I noticed the other day that they have a lot of left-
over prom dresses in there."

Cassie's face scrunched up like she had just sucked
on a lemon. "A prom dress as a *bridesmaid* dress?" She
snorted. "As if."

"Totally," Kayley agreed.

They looked at Samantha.

"Right," she added quickly. "Totally as if."

"Some of them are super fancy," I retorted. "Especially with the right jewelry." The bridesmaid dresses
I had seen in magazines were all so boring looking. At
least something from Forever 21 would be interesting.
Plus, I was all about mixing things up. Like how I used
a cat dish from Petco with a crown on it to hold some
of my jewelry.

"Not to mention Forever 21 is so—" Cassie started to say.

"So what?" I demanded. "Isn't that purple shirt you were wearing when I was over your house the other day from there? I'm pretty sure I saw it in the store window when I walked by this week."

Her face got red. "Yes, but I wouldn't buy a *bridesmaid* dress there."

Lana gave her a look and turned back to me. "Avery, I think that sounds like a really creative idea . . ."

I brightened. At least someone here didn't think I was a total loser.

". . . but I was thinking we'd try Saks first and see if they had something that worked."

"Saks Fifth Avenue?" I asked. I had been in there only once, when I had to pee so bad after drinking a giant lemonade slushy from the food court that I could barely walk. When I saw that a pair of socks cost fifty bucks, I got so nervous that I ran out of there as fast as I could. Mom explained to me that the reason they were so expensive was because they were made out of cashmere. Even if they were made out of gold, fifty dollars was a lot of money for something that was just going to end up smelling.

"No. Saks *Third* Avenue," Cassie replied.

"That's *enough*, Cassie," Lana snapped as she shot her a look. She made sure to put her smile back on before turning to me. "Because it's such a special occasion, I thought we could splurge." Dad had already told Mom that he'd pay for my dress.

"Oh, I love Saks. I go there all the time," I lied. I just hoped no one would ask me where the juniors department was. I picked up the tray of drinks. "I got these for us."

"That was so thoughtful of you," Lana said.

"Yeah," Cassie agreed. "It was."

I couldn't believe it! *Finally* I had done something right in Cassie's mind.

"Too bad with all your *experience* in stores like Saks you forgot that you can't bring drinks in there," she went on.

"You can't? I don't remember seeing a sign last

time I was there . . . ," I said. I knew I hadn't, because I'd still had some of my lemonade left and didn't want to throw it out, so I had looked.

"It's just something that people who shop in those kinds of places know is a faux pas," Kayley added.

I wasn't sure what that meant, but I had a feeling it wasn't good.

Lana looked at her watch. "Unfortunately, we don't have a lot of time, so we can't really hang out here and drink them. But I'm sure we'll need something when we're done, so we can get more then." She picked up the tray. "I'll bring them back to Starbucks. Maybe the baristas would like them."

"It's okay—I'll do it," I said quickly, taking the tray from her. "I'll be right back."

But instead of going to Starbucks, I walked over to Claire's and offered the drinks to the salesgirls there. Claire's was my second-favorite store in the mall after Forever 21. Obviously, I preferred making my own jewelry, but I had gotten a lot of stuff from there as well.

Like anyone would be, they were psyched to have

four free Frappuccinos and told me how nice I was to think of them. (Not a bad thing to have the people who worked at a store you went to a lot think you were nice and generous.) The fifth drink I held on to because there was no way I was throwing mine out. After looking at Cassie's sour puss all this time, I needed something sweet. Standing near the entrance of the store, I peered out to make sure they were all still at the fountain. Then I checked to make sure the lid was on tight and stuck the drink in my bag.

"All set?" Lana asked when I got back to the fountain.

"Yup," I said with a smile, clutching my bag tightly. Luckily, I had brought my tote bag that had a map of Paris on it that day. It was one of my better garage sale finds, and the fact that it was a tall bag with a snap on top made it so I could fit the drink in it and no one could see inside.

As we walked through Saks to the formal-wear department, I saw that it wasn't just their socks that were expensive—everything was. I saw one dress with a price tag for two thousand dollars! But I had to admit that I could understand why it all cost so much—everything was super beautiful. Plus, you could tell it wasn't going to fall apart in the washing machine like a lot of the stuff from Forever 21 and H&M.

Lana told us that we should each pick out two dresses that we liked, and we'd all try them on and vote. I actually found, like, five dresses I liked, but I didn't want to be greedy. Even though Lana said not to worry about the price, I made sure not to choose something more than two hundred dollars. Kayley, on the other hand, seemed to think her new last name was going to be Kardashian—one of the dresses she chose was five hundred dollars. When Lana saw the price tag, she immediately ordered her to put it back. Which was a good thing, because all the tulle on it made it so poufy we would have looked like a family of ungraceful ballerinas.

After we all chose our dresses, the saleswoman brought us back to a lounge area, where she spread the eight dresses out on the couches and seats that were out there so we could see them side by side.

"Well, we've got a real cross-section of styles

here," she announced, trying to sound excited but sounding bored instead. Like a lot of the people who worked there, she was dressed all in black with very high heels. Between her shoes and the way her blond hair was pulled back into such a tight bun, I could understand why she barely smiled—she was probably in a ton of pain.

Just looking at the dresses, you could see how different our tastes were. Both of Cassie's dresses had so much beading that they must have weighed thirty pounds each. Kayley's were more appropriate for a funeral than a wedding because they were both black. Sammi—maybe because she was sick of Cassie yelling at her to hurry up—had picked two that looked like you'd wear them to work in an office job.

Cassie pointed to the fuchsia minidress with hibiscuses splashed across it that I had chosen. "Does that one come with sunglasses?" she asked innocently. Kayley giggled.

I gave her a dirty look. Although I was trying my hardest to suck it up and not let her get to me, I was at the point where I couldn't handle much more.

Especially because when I showed Lana my other choice—a turquoise silk shift that had little pearls on the spaghetti straps and neckline—I heard Kayley whisper to Cassie that it looked like a nightgown.

"I think it's neat," said Sammi.

I gave her a grateful smile. Maybe there was hope for this to work out. Having only two out of three of my stepsisters hate me wouldn't be *that* bad.

"You would," said Kayley. "You don't have any taste."

"Okay, that's enough," Lana said sternly, before turning to the saleswoman. "Can you check to see if you have all these in the girls' sizes?"

"Of course," she said. "I'd be more than happy to."

"How come she looks like she just sucked on a lemon?" Sammi asked as the saleswoman click-clacked away.

"I know, right? Maybe her hair's pulled too tight," I said.

She giggled.

This was great! The two of us were on our way to having our own private jokes!

I was still walking on air a few minutes later as we

made our way to the dressing rooms. The dresses were already hanging on hooks, and in each dressing room there was a pink slipcovered chair that looked so comfortable it made me want to take a nap. Instead I placed my tote bag down and, after making sure the door was locked, took out my drink to take a sip.

"Girls?" I heard Lana call from outside the room.

Good thing I had locked the door. "Mmm-hmmm," I replied, my mouth full of Frappuccino.

"I want you to try on the turquoise dress first and come out so we can look at them all together," she said.

"Why do we have to start with one of *her* choices?" Cassie demanded from the room next to mine.

"Yeah," Kayley echoed. Even though there were enough dressing rooms that we all could have had our own, the two of them had decided to share one. It was definitely big enough.

There was so little space at the bottom of the partition that there was no way either of them would be able to peek through, but I was still nervous they'd see my drink, so I quickly put it back in my bag on the chair and closed the snap. As I got undressed, I got a little sad listening to the two of them joking around together. As jerky as they had been to me so far, I kept hoping that something would make them stop hating me and we'd all get along.

I got out my iPhone and took a picture of the dresses and texted it to Lexi.

this would be so much more fun if u were here, I wrote.

OMG THAT IS SOOOOOO BEAUTIFUL!!!! ARE YOU HAVING THE BEST TIME???? she wrote back almost immediately.

I wished I was one of those people who could lie about how she was feeling, but I wasn't. not really, I replied. i'm actually kind of lonely ☹

UGH. THE BB'S ARE AT IT AGAIN????

yeah. k gotta go. luv ya.

LUV YA 222222222 XOXOXOXOXO

Lexi's *Xs* and *Os* made me smile. We might not have been related, but I felt like we were sisters. At least I'd always have her. Mom liked to say that friends were the family you got to choose.

Love you Like a Sister

As soon as I put the dress on, I could see that my talent for finding great stuff had struck again. Not only was it supersoft against my skin because it was silk, but it fell in such a way that it made me look like I had boobs even though I was flat as a pancake. There was something to be said for expensive stuff. As I looked at myself in the three-way mirror, I felt like a character in a Disney sitcom after she gets made over. Which was fun.

Or *would* have been fun, if I'd had someone to share it with.

I took my Frappuccino out of my bag and sipped at it. I could see how being a bridesmaid and helping to plan a wedding could be a great time, but not if it was going to keep being like this—where all my ideas were shot down, and the BBs made it clear whenever they could that, no matter what, I'd always be their stepsister versus their real sister.

"Are you girls ready?" Lana called from outside the dressing room. "Come show us."

I opened my dressing room at the same time as Cassie and Kayley. "Wow. Those look great on

♥ 97 ♥

you two," I said. Kayley leaned forward. "Is that a *Frappuccino* in your bag?" she said loudly.

I turned to look. How could I have been so dumb and not fastened the snap?! Cassie's eyes narrowed. "You were supposed to throw that out."

"I know. I just . . . ," I sputtered nervously. "I get really thirsty when I shop. . . ."

As the two of them stared at me, I knew that no matter what excuse I came up with, I was still busted. "Please don't tell your mom," I begged. The last thing I needed was for Lana to think I was a liar and a sneak. Which, essentially, I was by having done this.

"What's in it for us?" Cassie demanded.

"Whatever you want," I said quickly. The minute the words left my mouth, I cringed. What was I getting myself into?!

Sammi came out of her room. "What's going on?"

"Nothing," I said quickly.

Before they could tell her, Lana called for us again. "We'll think about it and get back to you," Cassie replied.

"You'll think about what?" Sammi asked.

"Don't worry about it," Kayley told her.

As we modeled the dress for Lana, I felt like I was going to throw up. It would be horrible if they told her about the drink, but knowing I was about to be black-mailed was even worse.

"I like it a lot," Lana said as we stood in front of her. "Let me—"

"Okay, great," I said quickly as I spun around to go back to the dressing room.

"Wait a minute. Let me see the back," she went on.

I stopped quickly so Lana could examine the back. "This is the back. It's a nice back, don't you think?" I babbled. I picked up the skirt and kept on going into the dressing room. "Okay, I'm going to go change now!"

Out of the corner of my eye I could see she was confused. Every time I went back to the dressing room, I checked my bag to make sure the drink was still there. I would've thrown it out, but there were no garbage cans to be seen. I wondered what you were supposed to do if you wanted to spit out your gum. But I guess if they didn't want you bringing drinks into a place like this, they probably didn't like gumchewers either.

I did feel a little better once I put the fuchsia dress on. It was beautiful. Superbright, but not obnoxiously so. And I already knew exactly what necklace I'd wear with it if we chose this one: a choker made of silver beads with a white quartz gardenia in the middle that I had made last year and always got a ton of compliments on. Not that we'd end up getting it—I was sure Cassie would have a bunch of reasons why she hated it.

"Ready?" Lana called out.

When I opened my dressing room door, Cassie and Kayley were already out in the hall. I waited for some comment about the dress, but they just ignored me. After making sure my door was closed tightly, so no one could go through my stuff, I joined them outside where Lana and the saleslady were waiting.

Holding my breath, I waited for Lana's response as she watched us model it.

"Well, it's definitely . . . *colorful*," she finally said.

It was. That's why it was so great. But I couldn't tell if she thought that was a good thing.

Finally she smiled. "I love it."

I exhaled. Score one for me! For a second I even forgot that I was about to be blackmailed.

She turned to the other girls. "What do you guys think?"

"I love it," Sammi said.

"I like it too," Kayley agreed.

Score two more for me!

We all looked over at Cassie.

She sighed. "Well, it's not *horrible*."

Score *ten* for me.

"Okay, then. I think we have our decision," Lana said. She turned to me. "Good job, Avery." She came over and grabbed the bottom of my hem. "I think it might be a touch too long on you and Sammi, though."

"I'll get the seamstress," the saleslady said as she click-clacked away.

I turned to Cassie. "I'm really glad you like the dress," I said shyly. "It looks great on you." It was probably stupid of me to keep trying with her, but I couldn't help it. The idea of having to go through not only this wedding planning with things the way they were with us, but then an entire lifetime after that, was enough to make me suck it up a bit longer in hopes she'd start being nice. Plus, maybe the blackmail wouldn't be so horrible.

"Well, it's a lot nicer on than it looks on the hanger," she said begrudgingly.

Before I could say anything else, the seamstress was there and turned me around so she could start pinning the hem.

Lana turned to the BBs. "Go get changed," she said.

After the seamstress was done, I walked back to the dressing room as carefully as possible in order to avoid getting jabbed in the legs. I felt great—better than I had since we had gotten here.

Until I saw that my dressing room door was open.

At that, my stomach started to do flips.

And then—after I got inside—it started to do flops as well.

The drink was still in my bag, but it was turned over on its side. Which meant that what was left of the now-melted Frappuccino—and there was a bunch left—was dripping out *ALL OVER THE DRESSES THAT I HAD HUNG OVER THE CHAIR.* I grabbed my own clothes and tried to do some damage control by mopping at the dresses in hopes of stopping the stains from getting bigger than they already were. "OH MY GOD . . . HOW DID THIS HAPPEN . . . I DIDN'T . . . ," I babbled wildly as I mopped away.

How had I knocked my bag over before I left?! I'd been so careful. . . .

Or had *someone else* come into the room and knocked the bag over *on purpose* while I was getting my dress hemmed?!

I guess I was pretty loud, because Lana and the saleswoman came running in.

"What's the matter?" the saleswoman cried. "Did someone rip one of the dresses?" Her eyes narrowed as she saw the now-empty cup. "Is that a . . . *coffee beverage*?" she demanded.

Everyone looked at me. "Um, yeah," I said nervously. "It is." The last of the gooey mess dripped onto the floor. "I mean, it *was*."

By this time a bunch of the other salespeople had gathered to see what the commotion was about. From the looks on their faces, you would have thought they were looking at roadkill rather than a spilled drink.

I looked over at the BBs. While it was obvious from the expression on Sammi's face that she felt bad for me, it was hard to tell what the other two were thinking. Although I could have sworn that there was a hint of a smirk on Kayley's face.

"I'm really, *really* sorry," I said. "But I'd just like to add that there was no sign saying that drinks aren't allowed—"

"That's because it would be self-explanatory to the type of clientele that we have in our store," the saleslady sniffed.

As I stood there praying for the floor to open and swallow me up, Lana examined the damage. I could see from the way she cringed that my hope that she wouldn't think it was *that* big of a deal was wishful thinking. "How did this happen, Avery?" she asked quietly.

The fact that she was calm rather than yelling at me made me feel even worse. "I don't know!" I cried. "I know you told me to get rid of the drinks . . . and I did . . . I mean, I got rid of four of them. . . ."

I cringed. This was *not* going well. "I didn't think it would be that big of a deal if I held on to mine . . . it was sitting upright before we went out to show you the dress. And then I wasn't here while I was getting my dress hemmed."

"What are you saying?" Cassie demanded. "That one of us went into your room and knocked it over *on purpose*?"

We stared at each other for a second. That was exactly what I was saying. Without actually saying it.

"No," I finally replied, my shoulders slumping. I couldn't do it. I couldn't accuse her in front of Lana. If I did, any chance of us getting along would be gone for good.

We had drawn quite the crowd by then, and I could see that Lana was getting more embarrassed by the second. "Well, regardless of how it happened, it needs to be taken care of," she said. She turned to a woman who was standing at the front. "I'm assuming you're the manager?"

The woman was so horrified her mouth made a little O as she nodded.

Lana rummaged in her purse for her wallet and took out a credit card. "If you could just charge the dry-cleaning bills for these dresses to this card, that would be great," she said as she held it toward the manager. She swallowed. "And of course we'll also be taking the four dresses we already picked out."

The manager grabbed the card and stormed off without a word.

"Lana, I'm *so* sorry," I whispered as my eyes started to sting with tears. "I really don't know how that happened."

"It's okay, Avery," she replied in a tight voice, making it seem like it was very far from okay.

"I can pay for the damage with my allowance," I offered. My allowance from, like, the next *fifty years*.

She put up her hand. "Let me just deal with this so we can get out of here."

"Okay," I mumbled.

But it wasn't okay.

None of it was.

Six

I think my dad felt really bad about our last car ride, because he went out of his way to ask if we could spend time together, just the two of us. Unfortunately, it was the day after Operation Frappuccino Fail.

I was so embarrassed about the whole thing that when he asked if I wanted to go for pizza, which was my favorite food in the entire world, I just shrugged and said, "I don't care," because I had no appetite at all. And I *always* had an appetite—*especially* when it came to pizza.

Because my grandmother called my dad during the drive over with a million questions about the wedding ("How many people are you inviting?" "Who are you seating us with?" "What are you serving as an entrée? I hope it's not steak, because they usually only cook it medium and I like mine medium well." "You remember that your father is allergic to shellfish, don't you?"), I was saved from a conversation about what had happened at the mall. And then, when we sat down in a booth at Pizzeria Pagano and ordered a large ham and pineapple (it turned out that it was both of our favorite pizza, so it must be hereditary), Lana called to say that the power had gone out, so he had to stay on the phone with her as she went to the fuse box. By the time she had gotten the power back on and they hung up, I was already on my second slice (apparently, my appetite had come back) and was hoping that maybe if I ate fast enough, I could get through dinner without having to talk about what had happened.

"Sorry about that," my dad said as he reached for a slice.

"It's okay," I replied. "If you want to call her back to make sure the power didn't go out again, I totally understand."

He gave me a strange look.

"Because sometimes it goes out again right away." I had no idea whether or not that was true, but it sounded like maybe it could have been.

"I'm sure it will be fine," he said as he pushed his phone away. "So. Let's talk about—"

"Isn't the pizza here good?" I interrupted.

"Yes. Very," he said.

"Mom and I like it the best out of all the Italian restaurants in town," I went on. That was saying a lot, because there were a ton of them.

"That's great. Now, about yesterday . . . ," he said before I could steer the conversation in another direction again.

I slumped down in my seat. "Yeah?"

"Let's talk about what happened at Saks."

"It wasn't my fault!" I cried. "I only bought the drinks because I wanted them to like me, and then they acted like I was stupid for doing so, and I swear I checked the top on the cup before I left the room, so there's no way it could have tipped over!"

"So you're saying that one of the girls went into

the dressing room and intentionally knocked your drink over."

I stared at him. "I didn't say that," I finally said. At least not *out loud*.

He tore off a little bit of the crust on his slice, which was exactly how I ate my pizza too. "Lana said that you were really upset about what happened."

"Well, yeah! Wouldn't you be if everyone accused you of ruining a bunch of really expensive dresses?"

"*Did* someone accuse you of doing that?" he asked gently.

I looked away. "Not, you know, *to my face*," I admitted. "But I know they were thinking that."

"Avery, I know that the girls can be a little . . . slow to warm up."

Warm up? It was like using a hair dryer on an iceberg.

"But you have to remember, this is just as tough for them . . . ," he went on.

"How?" I asked. "There's three of them, and they're already sisters, and have private jokes and really nice clothes."

He tipped his head down to look at the denim overalls that Mom had sewn into a jumper for me using fabric from one of her old Indian caftans that had fallen apart because it had been washed so much. Underneath it I was wearing a pink tank that I had painted a blue jay on. (Last year had been my "bird phase," as Mom called it, where I painted different birds all the time.) "From what I'm looking at, you have really nice clothes too."

"But none of this is new," I replied. "And when I told Cassie that I liked to get stuff at garage sales, she wrinkled her nose as if I had said I got my food out of garbage cans."

"You just have to give all of this time. We all do."

I opened my mouth to say something but decided against it.

"What is it, Avery?"

I sighed. "I just wish I was one of those people who knew how to be someone else, but I don't. I'd probably be really popular if I could do that."

"But why would you want to be someone else when who you are is already pretty great?" he asked.

I looked at him, surprised. Okay, I was not expecting my dad to say that. I mean, he barely knew me.

"Avery, sometimes when we're afraid, we need to act *as if*."

"What does that mean?"

"Well, it means we need to act *as if* we believe something's going to work out and *as if* there's nothing about ourselves we need to change, because who we are is already enough."

Why was I feeling like I was about to cry?

"Because when we do it long enough, sometimes it becomes the truth rather than something we hoped for."

I thought about it. It made some sense. Like when I decided I wanted to make jewelry, I never thought, *But how can I make jewelry? I'm just a kid*. I just acted as if it was totally normal and I did it. And sure enough, I became a jewelry designer . . . who just happened to be a kid.

"You need to remember that time takes time," he went on.

Wow. My dad was filled with weird sayings. "What does *that* mean?" I asked.

"It means that building a relationship with someone doesn't happen overnight," he explained. "You have to show up and put effort into it." He thought about it. "Like what I have to do with you."

He was right—things did take time. Like, as nice as it was that we were spending time together, I didn't quite trust it yet. How did I know that one day it wouldn't suddenly go back to how it had been the last ten years?

He must have seen something on my face, because just then he reached over and grabbed my hand. "Avery, I know I haven't been much of a father over the years—"

"I never said that," I interrupted.

"I know you didn't. But it's the truth," he sighed. "But meeting Lana, and seeing the relationship she has with her girls . . . it's made me see how much you've been shortchanged."

I hated the fact that I could feel my eyes getting wet. I did *not* want to cry in front of my dad. I shrugged. "It's not that big of a deal."

He squeezed my hand. "It's a huge deal, Avery, and I'm very, very sorry. And you're right—I've been so caught up in my life that I haven't focused on yours. Do you think we can start over?"

"What do you mean?"

"I mean . . . how about once a week we spend some time, just the two of us?"

"Really?"

He nodded. "Yeah. We can get to know each other again that way. Or more like, get to know each other finally."

I smiled. "I think that would be really nice."

Apparently, I wasn't the only one who was asked to try a little harder.

On Wednesday afternoon Lexi and I were in front of the bakery, pooling our money together to see if we had enough to buy a cupcake to split (then would come the hard part: deciding what to get, seeing that I was all about chocolate and she was one of those strange people who didn't like it), when my phone rang.

As I fished it out and we looked at the screen, my eyes widened. It was Cassie.

Lexi gasped. "Oh my *gosh*! Why is *she* calling *you*?"

"I don't know," I replied, baffled.

"Answer it! Answer it!" she cried as it continued to ring.

"I'm *going* to! Just calm down," I replied, nervous. That was, if I could get my fingers to work.

"I can't believe she's calling you. What do you think she wants? It's going to go to voice mail if you don't get it!" she babbled.

"*Shhh,*" I ordered as I punched accept on my phone. A little too hard, apparently, as it fell to the ground and skittered across the concrete.

"What are you doing? You're going to break it! Did you break it?"

It was a good thing she was already my best friend, because her annoyingness would have made it tough for her to find another. "Stop talking!" I cried as I picked it up. It was still ringing. "Hello?" I said after I answered. I tried to sound all calm, but I had a feeling I was failing.

"Hey, Avery. It's Cassie. How are you?"

"Oh, I'm *great*," I replied. "Just hanging out with my best friend, Lexi. Just, you know, doing . . . best-friend things . . . shopping, about to get a cupcake . . ." Okay, I really needed to shut up now.

Lexi leaned in. "Hi, Cassie. We've never met, but I've heard all about you," she yelled into the phone.

"What are you doing?!" I snapped as I moved away from her.

"I'm just trying to be friendly!" she snapped back.

"I won't keep you, then," Cassie said, sounding really bored. "I'm just calling because my mom—"

"Cassie," I heard Lana say in the background in a warning voice.

"Sorry—because *my sisters and I* thought you might want to get together and do something sometime."

Could she have sounded less excited about the idea?

"Oh. Sure. That sounds great," I replied. Could *I* have sounded less excited? Maybe I should have taken after Lexi and tried out for some plays in order to sharpen my acting skills.

"Okay. Well, I guess I'll see you at some point, then," she said. "Have a good day."

"Wait!" I said before she could hang up. "When do you want to do it?"

"Do what?"

"Hang out," I replied.

"Oh," she said, busted. I could already tell this was going to be a ton of fun. "Um . . . I need to check to see when I'm free."

Although I couldn't make out what Lana was saying in the background, I could tell from her tone she was annoyed. "My mom says we could do it tomorrow afternoon."

"Tomorrow afternoon works," I replied. The minute I said it, I cringed. I should have said I needed to check my schedule or something.

Lexi pulled on my arm. "But that's when we—"

I waved her off. "So what do you want to do?" I asked into the phone.

"I don't know," Cassie replied.

Lexi pulled on my arm again. "Tomorrow is when we planned on going to the art supply store—"

"Can't you see I'm on the phone?" I hissed. The minute it left my mouth, I felt bad, because it came out a lot more harsh than I had expected. I just wasn't a good multitasker, especially when I was nervous.

Which, when talking to Cassie, I always seemed to be. I turned away so I didn't have to look at the hurt look on her face, and cleared my throat. "There's this neat store near my house on Main Street called You Are Here. How about we meet there at, like, two?"

"Okay. See you tomorrow."

Before I could say anything else, she ended the call. Which was fine because it wasn't like I could think of anything else to say. And even if I could, I would have saved it up for the next day so there would be only 299 awkward silences instead of 300.

When I turned toward Lexi, I could see she was still upset. "I'm sorry. That was really rude of me."

"Yeah. It was," she agreed, hurt.

I felt bad. Although Lexi hadn't said anything, I had been able to tell from the look on her face earlier when I told her about my conversation at the pizza place with my dad that this was all tough for her. One of the first things we had bonded over when we became friends was the fact that our fathers weren't around, and now not only was mine here, but he was making a big effort to make up for the years that he wasn't.

"It's like you're willing to drop everything for these girls who—no offense—have been nothing but total jerks to you so far."

Okay, that was tough to swallow. Probably because it was true. "I have an idea," I said. "Do you want to come tomorrow?"

At that she brightened. "Omigod, REALLY?!" she gasped.

"Uh-huh," I replied.

She started to hop on one foot, which was a sign she was *really* excited.

"Unless you want me to call her back and tell her I forgot I had plans already."

"No way!" she yelled. "We can get art supplies ANYTIME!" She stopped hopping and gave me a huge hug. "This is going to be soooo cool!"

"Totally," I agreed with a smile, hoping I looked a lot less nervous than I felt.

seven

The next afternoon, as I stood in front of You
Are Here at 1:45 (when I got nervous, my earliness
kicked in), my jaw dropped as I watched Lexi chain up
her bike and cross Main Street to meet me.

"What do you think? Do I look okay?" she asked
striking a pose.

"I need to get my sunglasses out before I can
answer that question," I said, shielding my eyes.
Between her dangly rhinestone earrings, the
bedazzled rose on her T-shirt, and the fake diamond
flower on her sandals, I could barely see. "*What* are

you wearing? You said in your text you were wearing your denim mini and a pink tank top!"

"I know, but then I thought it might make you look better if they thought you had a best friend who was really sophisticated," she replied, "so I changed." She put her hand on her hip and struck a pose like a model. "What do you think?"

I couldn't bear to tell her the truth, (a) because I didn't want to hurt her feelings, and (b) because it was too late for her to go home and change. "I think you look . . . really sparkly." At least it wasn't a lie.

She smiled. "Thanks. That was the look I was going for."

Before I could say anything else, Lana's car pulled up. Because the windows were closed, I couldn't hear, but I could see Lana say something to the girls before she turned the ignition off and they all got out.

"Hey, Avery!" she chirped. She stayed over near the door and didn't hug me this time, which made me think that maybe she was still mad at me about the dress, even though my dad had said she wasn't. But I didn't have time to think about that right then.

"Hey, Lana." I pulled Lexi so she was beside me. "This is Lexi."

"It's such a pleasure to meet you, ma'am," she said.

I gave her a look. *Ma'am?* When had Lexi ever used the word "ma'am" before? Later on when I asked her about it, she told me she thought that Lana might be impressed by it, seeing that she was from California. Which didn't make much sense to me, but then again, lots of what Lexi said often didn't make sense.

"You too, Lexi," Lana replied. "I have to run to a doctor's appointment, but I'll be back here at five. That should give you girls enough time to hang out, right?"

"You could even come at four thirty, if you wanted," Cassie said.

"Five it is," Lana said, ignoring her. "Have a great time." She looked at me. "Avery, I gave Cassie some money for all of you to get a snack."

"Yeah. Maybe we can get Frappuccinos," Kayley murmured. Cassie tried not to laugh.

"Thanks," I said, trying not to glare at Kayley.

"Mom, I bet I can find something blue around here," Sammi said.

Lana smiled. "I bet you can too."

"I'll help you look, if you want," I offered.

Sammi looked at her sisters, as if checking to see what they thought, but they looked just as bored as usual. She turned to me. "Okay."

I smiled at her.

"I'll help too," Lexi added. "I *love* blue. I even have blue eye shadow."

I was surprised she wasn't wearing it, because it was also really sparkly.

"I bet that's neat," Sammi said.

"It totally is," Lexi replied. I had a feeling they'd end up being good friends before the day was over.

I turned to Kayley. "I know you said you don't need any help finding something new for your mom, but they have a lot of cool stuff in here."

She shrugged. "Okay."

That was easy enough. Hopefully, the next two hours would be as well.

Luckily, Maryam—Mom's friend—was working

that day. She was originally from Iran and was super-cool. I especially liked her English accent, which she had because she had gone to primary school in England (that's what they call elementary school there). She was so cool that she let me put my jewelry in her display case, and if anyone bought some, we'd split it fifty-fifty. So far nothing had sold, but it still made me feel good when I walked in and saw it there.

"Look what the cat dragged in," Maryam said when she saw us. Her hair—which had purple streaks in it today, as opposed to pink or green or blue, which she had also had on occasion—was pulled back into a ponytail, making her hoop nose ring stand out even more. There was a lot going on with Maryam, one of the things I liked about her so much. Her eyebrows went up as she took in Lexi's outfit. "Lexi, you're looking quite dazzling today. Literally."

"Thanks," Lexi replied. "It's just something I threw on really fast without thinking about it."

Yeah, right.

"Well, excellent job." She turned to the BBs. "Hi. I'm Maryam."

I could tell from the looks on their faces that they weren't quite sure what to make of her. Maybe they didn't have purple hair in California.

"Why is your hair like that?" Sammi asked.

"Sammi!" Cassie said, embarrassed.

Maryam laughed. "It's okay. My mum asks me the same thing every time she sees me." She came over and leaned down so she was eye to eye with Sammi. "My hair is like this because I like the way it looks."

Sammi moved behind me. I smiled and patted her on the shoulder. I loved that she had chosen *me* to hide behind!

"Come here, Sammi," Kayley said.

Sammi went over next to her sister—her *real* sister— who made a big show of putting her arm around her.

"These are my dad's fiancée's daughters," I said to Maryam. I couldn't bring myself to call them my soon-to-be stepsisters right then. And not just because they technically weren't yet.

"They're from California," Lexi added. The way she said it made it sound like that explained everything.

"Ah. This must be a big change for you all," Maryam said.

"You can say that again," Cassie replied with a bored sigh as she started looking at the bags hanging on the wall.

Maryam looked at me and raised one eyebrow just the tiniest bit, which I took as code for *Oh boy, do I feel sorry for you.*

"We're in charge of finding something old, new, and blue for Lana—she's the bride," I explained, "and I thought this would be a good place to start."

"I'm honored," Maryam replied. "Take your time looking around and let me know if you need any help."

There was nothing old in the shop, so that saved me from having to deal with Cassie. Which was probably good, seeing that she was busy looking for things for herself anyway.

I turned to Sammi. "Should we try and find something blue?"

"Yeah!"

I smiled at her and decided to push my luck by taking her hand to lead her over to the glass case where the jewelry was. Maybe we'd find a pair of earrings with a blue stone.

Kayley was already over there. When I saw what she was looking at, my face got red. There, behind the glass, was a necklace I had made out of sea glass I had found when Mom and I went to Maine last summer.

Lexi came over and pointed at it. "See that one with the sea glass?"

Uh-oh.

"Yeah. It's neat," Kayley said. "It's so . . . different."

I cringed. So much for having time to figure out how to tell her it was mine.

"That's funny you should say that, because the designer is in this *very shop* at this *very moment*."

I cringed some more.

Kayley looked around. "Really? Where?"

I shook my head at Lexi and mouthed, "Stop it!"

"Right next to you," Lexi replied.

Kayley turned and looked at me. Busted.

"*You* made that?" she asked.

"Yeah?" I squeaked.

By this time Cassie had wandered over and was peering at it. "That necklace? Really?"

"Uh-huh?" Why was everything I said coming out as a question?

"I can't believe you make jewelry," Kayley said.

Was it my imagination or did she sound impressed?

I shrugged. "I've made a few things."

"A *few*?" said Lexi. "Try, like, *fifty*."

It was nearly impossible to lie when Lexi was around.

"Wow," said Kayley.

This time there was no mistaking it—she *was* impressed.

"Oh, it's totally wow," agreed Lexi. "She makes necklaces, and earrings and bracelets." She put her hand on my arm to steady herself and started hopping on her left foot as she lifted her right leg. "She even made this anklet for me for my birthday. And because it's the only anklet she's made, that makes it extra exclusive."

Kayley turned to Cassie. "Neat, huh?"

Cassie shrugged before turning to examine the

scarves. "Well, yeah, I guess it would be if it was, like, the first jewelry designer you had ever met. But there's, like, a *ton* in California."

However many inches Kayley's reaction had added to my height disappeared as my shoulders slumped. Kayley gave her a look. "When did you ever meet a jewelry designer?"

Now it was Cassie's turn to blush. "I've met a bunch. You don't know them."

Whether or not that was true, I decided to focus on the positive stuff—like the idea that Kayley thought I was cool. Or at least my jewelry was cool, which, because I was the one who made it, made me cool by association. "I'm hoping to get an Etsy shop set up," I confessed.

"I love Etsy!" she said.

"Me too."

"Do you have a website or anything with your stuff?" she asked.

I shook my head. "No. But I have pictures."

"Maybe there's something that my mom could use as her something new."

I couldn't believe she had said that! That's what *I* had wanted to say but couldn't get my nerve up. I nodded as if mulling it over. "Sure. We might be able to find something. Or if you have some ideas of what she'd like, I could just make it."

She smiled. "That would be awesome."

Lexi stuck her head into the conversation. "She usually charges extra for custom-made stuff."

Okay, (a) I had never custom-made anything before, and (b) I was going to kill her.

I smiled back. I actually had an idea that would take care of the something new *and* the something old, but I was worried that I might be pushing my luck. Especially since Cassie would be included in the decision.

The next two hours weren't so bad. A few doors down we found a tiny blue hand-painted turtle at a pottery store that Sammi got for Lana because (a) it was blue and (b) Lana loved turtles. (According to Kayley, that was not quite true. What had happened was one day on the way home from gymnastics, Sammi had said, "Mom, do you like turtles?" and Lana had said,

"I've never really thought about it, but I guess they're all right," which had somehow turned into Lana liking turtles.) When I told her I could make it into a pin for her mom if she wanted, she went nuts. Across the street from there, in this store called Origami (there wasn't actually any origami in the store—Marc, the owner, just liked how it sounded), Cassie bought a cover for her phone and Lexi debated for the millionth time about whether to use her allowance that she had saved up for this red patent-leather bag that was so big she would have been able to carry around not just her textbooks, but the entire grade's. After that it was Cassie who suggested we stop at Javalicious. Maybe it was because the Chillsies there were so good, but she even cracked a smile when Lexi told her story about losing her bikini top during our class trip to the Jersey shore last year and having to wait in the ocean until I brought her a shirt.

"So when you lived in California, did you get to meet movie stars and stuff?" Lexi asked. She turned to me. "That's where most of them live," she explained, as if I lived under a rock.

"We didn't live in Los Angeles. We lived up north near San Francisco," Kayley replied.

"There's movie stars up there, too," Cassie said.

"So did you meet any?" Lexi asked again.

"Well, no," Cassie admitted. "But my best friend was on vacation in New York City last year, and she saw Taylor Swift walking her dog."

"Wow," I said. "Taylor's awesome. She's the first Instagram I check in the morning."

"She's okay," Cassie said, with a shrug.

I just couldn't win. If I had said I didn't really like Taylor, I bet Cassie would have said she was her favorite singer ever.

"So we need to focus on the something-old thing," she said.

I nodded. "I know you don't like thrift stores, but there's one right across the street that has some cool stuff, so I was thinking maybe we could check it out."

She shrugged. "Whatever."

Timeless Treasures was my favorite store on Main Street. One of the things that was neat about it was that they had special sections labeled SIXTIES,

SEVENTIES, EIGHTIES, and NINETIES. I liked the stuff from the seventies the best. But they also had a big selection of jewelry and accessories, which was where Cassie and I started looking, while Kayley, Lexi, and Sammi poked around in the clothes.

"What do you think about this?" I asked, holding up a thin silver necklace with a butterfly. I loved butterflies. They were all over my room. I once even had a quilt that was covered with them. "Butterflies are good luck." I wasn't quite sure about that, but it sounded good.

The look on her face was enough to let me know it was a no. "Okay, then. I guess it's a no." Maybe we could just each get Lana something old separately so we didn't have to deal with each other.

Cassie walked over to the seventies rack and started flipping through it. "So you actually wear stuff from here?"

I joined her. "Yeah. All the time." As I went through the clothes, I came upon a paisley blouse and plucked it off the rack. I then moved over to where the jeans were. "What size jeans do you wear?"

"Twenty-five. Why?" she said suspiciously.

My eyes brightened. "Perfect." I did too, so I had a good sense of what was in that section. As I flipped through there, I found them—a pair of dark denim bell-bottoms that had an *O* on one back pocket and a *K* on the other. I had been stalking them for weeks. I picked them up and turned to Cassie. "Try these on," I ordered, handing her the jeans and the blouse.

"I don't know," she said doubtfully.

"There was a photo on Instagram last week of Taylor Swift wearing an outfit almost exactly like this," I said. That wasn't entirely true. I had seen a photo of her in bell-bottoms at one point, but it might have been a year ago. And she wore lots of blouses, but I wasn't sure any of them were actually paisley. That being said, I knew that this particular outfit was a great combination, because I had tried it on myself.

She walked over and took it from me. "Fine. But I'm trying it on because I like it. Not because I want to dress like a celebrity or anything."

As she changed in the dressing room, Lexi came up to me. "What are you doing?" she whispered.

"You've been saving up to buy that outfit."

I shrugged. "So?"

"So by telling her to try it on, you're pretty much giving her permission to buy it."

"Maybe I've changed my mind," I replied. But that was a lie. The truth was, even though Cassie was continuing to be a jerk to me, I still wanted her to like me. I hated admitting that, because it made me look stupid, but it was true. It was like I couldn't help myself. And it wasn't all about wanting her to like me. It also had do to with my dad and Lana—wanting things to be easier for them.

But even though I didn't say that to Lexi, she already knew because we were best friends. Which made the look she gave me—kind of like the one you give your cat when she throws up on your favorite sweater, one of total disappointment—that much more difficult to swallow.

Just then the curtain opened and Cassie walked out.

"Wow, that looks *awesome* on you," Lexi said. She turned to me. "I actually think I like it better on her than you," she whispered.

"Gee, thanks," I said. I hated to admit it, but it did look a lot better on her than it did on me. Luckily, Lexi decided to go take a peek at the shoes. As Cassie stood in front of the mirror looking at herself from all angles, I waited. Finally I couldn't control myself. "What do you think?" I asked.

"I think . . . it's . . . interesting."

Okay, "interesting" wasn't "Oh my gosh, Avery, you have crazy-great taste and I want you to be my personal shopper," but it would do.

I walked over to where the purses were and grabbed a brown suede one with fringe. I had a similar one at home. "Here—try this with it," I said as I handed it to her.

She put it on her shoulder and turned toward the mirror. She nodded slowly. "This could work."

This *could* work? It made the outfit! "Okay, well, thanks for trying it on," I said. "I'm going to go look at the cowboy boots with Lexi."

To say that I was surprised when I saw Cassie bring the outfit and the bag up to the counter to buy them when she came out of the dressing room was an understatement. I joined her at the counter but didn't say anything.

As the woman handed her a bag with all of her new finds tucked inside, Cassie turned to me. "I think it's time to go back and meet my mom."

"Yeah."

I turned to head toward the door.

"You have good taste."

She said it so quietly that someone who didn't have supersonic hearing like I did probably would have missed it.

"Thanks," I said with a small smile.

Maybe there was hope after all.

Eight

♫

One of the things I loved most about my mom was how friendly she was. While she might not have been like Lexi's mom with stray animals, she was definitely a fan of stray people. ("There's no such thing as strangers, Avery. Only new friends you haven't met yet.") On Thanksgiving and Christmas our house was filled with people who weren't spending it with their families. Mom loved to entertain, and even though she couldn't cook, she was great at picking out foods at Trader Joe's. I didn't know if other kids had things like baba ghanoush and baked ziti and cucumber soup for Thanksgiving, but I did.

"I was thinking it's been a while since we had people over for dinner," she said a few mornings later after I came downstairs for breakfast. She was at the table with the coffee mug I had given her for Mother's Day that year—the one that said "One Sip at a Time." I knew she had to be on her second cup because she never started conversations before then.

"That would be fun," I said as I reached for the loaf of raisin bread we had gotten at the farmers' market a few days before. I loved raisin bread. Especially this one because it was so cinnamony and gooey that you didn't even have to put any butter on it, but I always put apple butter on it anyway. That way I could say I had had two servings of fruit for breakfast. "Who are you going to invite? Rachel and Ibrahim?" Rachel was also a professor and a good friend of Mom's. Her boyfriend was this guy named Ibrahim, who was originally from Egypt but had grown up mostly in Paris, so he had a French accent.

"No. I was thinking . . . some new people," she said as she tore off a piece of my bread when I joined her at the table.

"That couple you met at the food co-op during your shift last week?" I asked. "The ones who just moved here from Vermont?" If you were a member of the co-op, you could volunteer to work there and get discounts. I think Mom did it more because she liked talking to people than because she wanted to save money.

"Nope. But I would like to have them over at some point," she said. "I was thinking . . . your dad and Lana and the girls."

I stopped midbite. "For real?"

"Yes, for real," she said. "You're about to drip apple butter all over you."

I gulped down the toast so that wouldn't happen. I was wearing my favorite T-shirt—one of Mom's that she had gotten at a Billy Idol concert in the eighties—and it had been washed so many times that I was afraid it would fall apart the next time it came out of the dryer. "But . . . *why*?" I asked after my mouth was no longer full.

"Why?" she repeated. "It's more like 'Why not?' They're your new family, and I'd like to get to know them better."

My stomach did a flip-flop at the word "family." Even though we were planning a wedding, I almost kept forgetting that things weren't going to end there. That the wedding was just the beginning . . . of *the rest of my life* being attached to these people. Which, when I thought about it, freaked me out. Which was why I didn't let myself think about it unless it was pointed out to me. Like, say, now.

"Plus, you were complaining about how uncomfortable you felt in their house—maybe things will feel different when you have them in yours," she went on. "They can see more of who you are."

I looked out the kitchen into the living room, taking it in not as the person who lived here, but as a stranger. Mismatched overstuffed chairs that were fraying at the arms. A couch that we called the Leaning Sofa of New York because two of the legs were shorter than the others, so it slanted downward. A bunch of different Moroccan-style rugs that we had found at yard sales or on eBay. Lots of dust bunnies because Mom hated to sweep and I had inherited that dislike from her. Personally, I loved our house. It wasn't big, and it wasn't fancy, but it was completely us: definitely not matchy-matchy, not stuck up, and a little off center, but not so much that it didn't work.

It was the complete opposite of my dad and Lana's place.

And, in a way, a complete opposite of *them*.

"So what do you think? Do you think it's a good idea?"

I looked at her. I wanted to tell her that it was a HORRIBLE idea. But she looked so hopeful. Like Lexi, when I was slowing down on my ice cream and she thought maybe I was done with it and she could have it.

"I think it's a great idea," I lied.

"Plus, I've been looking for an excuse to cook."

Okay, that? *Not* a good idea.

On Friday afternoon I found myself in front of my closet, throwing in there everything I didn't want the BBs to see, before dragging the slipcovered armchair that was supposed to be used for reading, but instead was used as a place to put my clothes when I was feeling too lazy to put them away, in front of it.

"But don't you need to get in your closet to get something out to wear tonight?" Lexi asked from over on the bed. The bed that she was *supposed* to be making but was instead lying on with her head hanging off the foot of it, almost touching the floor.

I stopped pushing the chair. "Oh yeah," I panted. "I didn't think about that." I dragged the chair back and plopped down into it.

"What are you going to wear?" she asked.

"Well, I was thinking—"

"I think you should wear your denim skirt with your red cowboy boots and the navy shirt with the embroidered sleeves you got at Forever 21 in the spring."

I thought about it. "That could work. But I was—"

"Oh! Oh! Wait! I have a better idea!" she shouted. "Your capri jeans with your lilac tank with a white shirt over it tied at the stomach."

This could go on for hours if I didn't put an end to it. "I'm wearing that purple tank dress I got a few weeks ago with my white braided belt and black sandals." All of which were in the closet.

She gasped. "That's *exactly* what I was going to say next! Are you sure you don't want me to stay?" she asked as I began yanking off my clothes.

"Well, I mean, of course I *want* you to stay," I half lied as I pulled on the dress. "It's just that my mom says it's a family thing."

Lexi pouted. "But I'm family too."

"*I* know that, and *you* know that, but I don't think my dad does." The truth was that as much as I considered Lexi family, I was already nervous enough about what *I* might say tonight, let alone having to worry about what *she* said.

I put on my belt and shoes. "How's this?"

She walked around me with her hand in her chin like she was judging a contest at a county fair. Finally she nodded. "It looks good."

"Great." I smiled. "I couldn't have done it without you."

"I know," she said as she turned to go. "Don't forget to send me texts during dinner!"

"Okay." That I could do. Setting up my iPhone so it faced the dinner table while I FaceTimed her so she could watch it in real time (her other idea) was not going to happen.

I was in the process of getting my necklace just right (a choker I had made that was a leather cord with turquoise stones tied to either end) when Mom popped her head in.

"You look beautiful, honey," she said.

I turned. So did she. She was wearing my favorite red-and-blue-print Indian dress, and she had her hair up in a messy bun. "You do too."

"Really? Are you sure this is okay?" she asked.

"Mom, are you nervous?" I asked.

"What? No. Of course not," she laughed. Nervously. "Why would I be nervous? I mean, it's just dinner. With your father. And his fiancée. And her three girls." Her shoulders sagged. "Okay, fine—I'm a *little* nervous. But it's okay. It'll be fine. Well, as long as I don't burn the dinner," she joked. Suddenly her eyes widened. "Oh my gosh. The ziti!" she yelped. She ran downstairs, and I followed.

She had decided on baked ziti after finding a recipe called Foolproof Ziti for Dummies. Our kitchen was always kind of messy, but it rarely had smoke in it, which it did when we got there.

We looked at each other.

"Maybe it's not burned," I suggested hopefully. "Maybe it's just at the point where the cheese is really, really gooey."

Mom sighed as she bravely made her way toward the stove. "You're the best daughter in the world for always putting a positive spin on things, but even I know the chances of that being the case are about as likely as me going a day without coffee."

As she went to open the oven door, I ran up behind her and put my hands on her shoulders for moral support.

She turned her head. "Ready?"

"Yeah."

With a deep breath she opened the oven, and the kitchen immediately became twice as smoky.

"Get the fire extinguisher!" she yelled over the angry beeping of the smoke alarm.

"We don't have one!" I yelled back. "And they don't get rid of smoke anyway!"

She ran around the kitchen opening the windows. "Good point!"

After we had opened every window downstairs and could see each other again, we stood in front of the ziti pan to examine the corpse. Every inch of it was charred.

"I don't understand," Mom said, holding the printed-out recipe. "The recipe says thirty-five minutes at four hundred fifty degrees."

I took it from her. "Nope. It says *forty-five* minutes at *three hundred fifty* degrees."

Mom grabbed it and squinted as she held it close to her face. "Oh. I guess that's what I get for not wearing my glasses."

I looked at the clock. Dad, Lana, and the girls were due to arrive in twenty minutes. "So what are we going to do?"

Mom thought about it. "I have an idea."

An hour later the seven of us were sitting around the living room, smiling at one another awkwardly.

"The pizza should be here any minute," Mom said.

Dad nodded. "Great, great. I'm starved."

She looked at the BBs. "And I promise you—it's definitely worth the wait." She turned to me. "Right, honey?"

"Oh yeah. It's the best in town," I agreed. "Maybe even in, like, *five* towns." But I was so nervous that I was both hungry and nauseous at the same time, with the nauseous feeling winning, which was probably going to stop me from eating.

Mom popped up from her seat. "I'm going to get us some more appetizers!"

"Monica, we're fine—" Dad started to say.

"Be right back!" she trilled as she ran out of the room.

She returned a moment later with a bag of potato chips and poured them into the bowl, on top of the tortilla chip crumbs we had been snacking on. I hoped this was the new bag and not the one that was a year old and therefore probably stale. She pushed the bowl toward the BBs. "Please. Have some."

I saw Lana give them a nudging nod, much like the kind Mom gave me when we were visiting my grandparents and my grandmother offered me some of her "world-famous" liver. I'm not sure what world she was talking about, but it had to be one where there weren't a lot of people, because that stuff was nasty.

Kayley reached into the bowl and picked up a chip. The minute she put it in her mouth, she cringed. That must have been the old bag.

"Aren't the salt and vinegar ones good?" Mom asked Kayley.

"Uh-huh," Kayley said with her mouth full. I knew that face. It was the *I'd do anything for a napkin right now so I can spit this out* one.

"I like that kind!" Sammi said as she reached into the bowl and took not one chip but, like, five. She popped a few in her mouth and started chewing, only to stop quickly. "Ick. They're *stale*."

"Sammi!" Lana said.

"Sorry, but they are!" Sammi cried.

Mom looked super embarrassed. In fact, everyone did. Luckily, right then the doorbell rang.

"The pizza's here!" Mom said, relieved. Both she and my dad got up at the same time, bumping into each other as they started toward the door.

"Let me get it," my dad said once they had untangled themselves.

"No way," Mom said.

"Please. I want to."

"Thanks, but I got this," Mom said. "It's the least I can do after burning dinner." She cringed. "Whoops. I hadn't mentioned that part until now, had I?"

"Oh, I burn dinner *all* the time," Lana said.

"You do? When?" Sammi asked, confused.

"Well, we happen to really love pizza," my dad said quickly. "So, as good as I bet your meal would've been, this will probably be just as delicious." He walked toward the door. "And it's my treat. I insist."

Mom held up her hands. "Okay, okay." As she watched my dad pay the pizza guy, she absentmindedly reached for a chip. Once she'd bitten down on it, she grimaced. "Ugh. These *are* stale."

I stood up to go set the table. The good news was that things could only get better after this.

And they did.

For a while.

Maybe it was all the warm, gooey cheese, or the way the bubbles in the crust melted in your mouth, but by the time dinner was over, whatever awkwardness there had been (and there had been *a lot*) had disappeared. It was so relaxed that when Mom said, "Hey, I have an idea—why don't we play charades?" instead of getting all freaked out, which was what I usually did when anyone suggested charades, I just shrugged and said, "Okay."

"Charades? Seriously?" Cassie said under her breath.

After writing phrases on slips of paper, we put them in my cowboy hat (found at a garage sale for two bucks—yay me) and decided that Sammi would be the first one to choose.

She looked at the piece of paper and squinted. "I can't read this—does it say 'Beauty and the Beast?'"

Kayley looked over her shoulder and rolled her eyes. "Way to give everyone a huge hint."

"What? I can't read it. The handwriting is really messy."

"That would be my handwriting," Mom said, looking a little embarrassed.

"It's not even that messy," Kayley said.

"It is too!" Sammi cried.

"Okay. That's enough," Lana said. Then she turned to my dad. "Honey, why don't you pick?"

My dad might have been really book smart (he'd gone to law school *and* business school after he graduated from college), but when it came to charades? Not so much. In fact, he might have been one of the worst charades players in the history of charades. He was even worse than Lexi, and that was hard to do.

"It's a . . . book!" Sammi yelled.

He shook his head and pantomimed again.

"TV show?" Kayley asked.

He shook his head again.

"Place?" Mom guessed.

He shook his head again and turned to Lana. "What's a good symbol for 'Don't Stop Believing'?"

"Now you just said it!" Lana cried.

He cringed. "Oh. Hm. I did, didn't I?"

That was pretty much how the game went. At least until Cassie was up.

"TV show!" Kayley yelled.

She shook her head.

"Place!" Mom guessed.

She shook her head again.

"Movie?" I asked. She nodded, giving me a semi-grateful half smile. I think she was just happy someone had finally figured it out. She held up five fingers.

"Four words!" Sammi yelled.

Kayley elbowed her. "Don't you know how to count?"

Cassie shook her head in frustration.

"Five words," I said.

She nodded and held up five fingers again.

"Fifth word."

She nodded so hard her hair bounced up and down. She pointed to the ceiling and used her finger to draw a figure.

"Ceiling?" my dad said.

"Rain?" Lana asked.

"Water damage from last year's snow?" Mom piped up.

We all looked at her like she was nuts.

"Sorry. I'm still a little obsessed with that," she said sheepishly.

"Stars," I guessed.

Cassie clapped and nodded.

"The Fault in Our Stars!"

"Yes!" she screamed, holding up her hand for a high five.

I gave her one. Immediately after, we both looked embarrassed that we had done something so . . . friend-like. But while we might have found it awkward, out of the corner of my eye I could see the adults smiling, as if that moment was the whole purpose of this dinner.

"What a team you two make," Mom said, smiling.

"You sure do," my dad agreed.

I shrugged. "I just have a lot of experience with charades."

"Me too," Cassie said.

Mom stood up. "Avery, why don't you show the girls your room while I put on some coffee and get dessert ready?" We had gone to Kaufman's Bakery and gotten one of their carrot cakes. I was kind of a carrot cake expert, and theirs was the best by far. Their cream cheese frosting was just the right amount of sweet.

Even though I had made sure to do a last-minute

check to confirm anything potentially embarrassing had been hidden from view (mainly my old stuffed animals that I couldn't bring myself to put away), as we went up the stairs, my stomach got all wonky.

"Your house is . . . different," Kayley said as each step let out its own particular squeak and groan.

"It's a hundred and four years old," I said.

"That's *old*," Sammi said.

"Tell me about it," I replied. I stopped in front of the guest room and pointed to the floor. "Look at how the floor slopes."

Cassie wrinkled her nose. "Is this place *safe*?"

"Of course it's safe," I said, offended. "It just has a lot of experience." That's what Mom always said about it. When we got to my room, I stood in front of the doorway and gave it one quick eyeballing before letting them in. "This is my room."

As they took it in, I tried to see it through their eyes. The walls were covered with pictures I had cut out from magazines, of clothes I thought were cool and places I wanted to go (Paris was at the top of my list, followed by Sweden). And of course there were photos of jewelry I liked. There were also a bunch of photos of cute animals (I was a sucker for YouTube videos, especially the ones where dogs were nursing kittens and things like that). Instead of hanging curtains on the windows, I had covered them with Indian tapestries that Mom and I had found at a flea market in New York City. (She had washed them, like, five times before she let me hang them up, on account of the fact that she was worried there might be bedbugs in them.) And then there were my mobiles. I had made them myself. Some were made of paper cutouts, but others had stuff I had picked up on my trips to the thrift store: (marbles, Christmas ornaments, beads I had strung together). I'd used fishing wire to hang them, which made it look like they were suspended in space, which was cool. I was really proud of them—almost as much as my jewelry.

"Where'd you get these mobiles?" Kayley asked, fingering a star made of pearls that I had found for almost nothing at an after-Christmas sale at a drugstore. "Etsy?"

Having someone compare my stuff to something

you could find on Etsy was the biggest compliment I could imagine. "Nope. I made them."

All three of them looked at me, surprised. *"Really?"* Sammi gasped. "Can you make me one?"

"Sure. I'd love to."

Kayley looked impressed. "You're super crafty."

I shrugged. "I just like to do it."

Cassie walked over to the vanity table that Mom and I had found on the side of the road and stripped down and painted purple. A bunch of my jewelry was on it. "And you made these, too?"

I nodded.

She raised her eyebrows but didn't say anything.

I had given what I was about to do a lot of thought and decided it was now or never. I took a deep breath. "I was thinking . . . I might know a way we could do the something-old/something-new thing together."

They waited for me to go on.

"I thought maybe we could make your mom a charm bracelet, with each piece representing someone in the family." It felt weird to say "family." I held up the huge plastic tub of charms I had collected over the years. "There might be stuff in here we could use, or, if not, we could go to a thrift store."

I waited for them to roll their eyes or give me another clue that they thought it was a stupid idea, but they didn't.

"I get that that would be the old part, but what would be new about it?" Cassie asked.

"The bracelet itself," I said.

Kayley nodded. "That makes sense."

"So what do you think?" I asked nervously. The question was for all of them, but it was Cassie I was looking at.

"I like it," Kayley said.

"Me too," Sammi added.

Kayley turned to her. "It doesn't matter if you like it—you already got the something-blue part."

"I'm still allowed to like it!" she cried.

We all waited for Cassie's reaction. I felt like she was purposely taking an extra-long time to answer. Finally she shrugged. "Whatever."

It wasn't the "What a great idea!" answer I had been hoping for, but it would do.

Nine

After that I started to get excited. I spent the next few days gathering up different charms. I found a high-heeled shoe that I thought would be fun to represent Cassie, because she was way into shoes. A few blue things for Sammi—a heart, a rose, and a moon. After finding out by reading Kayley's Facebook page that she liked to write stories, I remembered I had one of those old-fashioned quill pen charms that had come in a bag of charms I found at a thrift store. And for my dad I found a golf club, because he was a big golfer. For me, I was thinking of a paintbrush.

When he called me randomly on Wednesday afternoon and asked if I wanted to come over for dinner that evening, I didn't even hesitate—I said yes right away. As much as I loved my mom and we always had a great time together, the idea of having an actual family with a bunch of people in it felt really cool. When he picked me up at five, I spent most of the ride going on about the charm bracelet. When we were a few blocks away, I stopped talking.

He glanced over at me. "What's the matter?"

"I've spent the whole time talking," I said, surprised. "Sorry about that."

"Why are you sorry?"

I shrugged. "I don't know. Because *you* didn't get to talk."

"Well, I'd say that's a good thing," he laughed. He grabbed my hand. "Avery, I want to hear about your life, and the stuff you're interested in and excited about."

My face got hot. "You do?"

"Of course I do!" He sighed. "I've missed out on too many years of not hearing about it."

I smiled. "Okay. But only if I can hear about you, too. It's only fair."

"Deal," he said, squeezing my hand.

Before dinner we all gathered in Cassie's room so I could show them the charms, as well as the sketch I had done of the bracelet. My idea was to use this thin, almost invisible wire so it looked like the charms were just suspended in space. Luckily, they liked the idea and the charms. If they hadn't, I wasn't sure what I would have come up with.

This time we had a real dinner instead of stale chips and pizza. Lana had made a big salad with avocado, which was my favorite fruit (most people mistakenly think it's a vegetable, but it isn't—it's a fruit), and a tomato pie. I had had apple pie before, and blueberry, and banana cream pie, but never a tomato one. When I told her that, she explained that tomato pie was very popular in the South, where she had grown up. I wasn't a big fan of tomatoes, but I did love cheese, and there was a lot of that in the pie.

During dinner Lana told us how she and my dad

had spent the afternoon with the caterer doing tastings of different hors d'oeuvres and main courses. They hadn't had enough time to do cake tastings, so Lana said that when it was time for that, we girls could go with her if we wanted. I definitely wanted to, because I loved cake almost as much as I loved Ben & Jerry's Chunky Monkey ice cream. As we were eating dessert (bread pudding with vanilla ice cream), Cassie announced she had an idea.

"Oh yeah? What's that?" Lana asked.

"I was thinking that maybe we could do a girls' spa day before the wedding," she said. "You know, facials, mani-pedis, massages . . . that kind of thing."

"That sounds terrific!" Lana replied. I think she was so happy that Cassie was finally showing some interest that she would have had the same reaction to her saying "I think we should all go climb a tree!"

"When we were shopping near Avery's house, I noticed a spa," she went on. "I think it was called Serenity something."

"Oasis of Serenity," I said, and nodded.

Lana turned to me. "Have you been there? Is it nice?"

"It's *really* nice," I replied. I left out the part about how it was really expensive. A mani-pedi was seventy-five bucks there, when it was only forty at Exceptional Nails near the mall. "A bunch of my mom's friends pitched in and got her a gift certificate there for her birthday for a day of beauty."

"It sounds like your mom has great friends," said Lana. She sounded a little sad. I realized that she didn't talk all that much about her own friends. Only two were coming to the wedding. Maybe she didn't have a lot.

I nodded. "She does. And she let me have the mani-pedi part because she doesn't like to get her nails done because she says it's a waste of money because they chip as soon as she works in the garden." As soon as I said that, I wished I could take it back. I didn't know if Mom would appreciate me telling people that. I loved the fact that she was so down-to-earth and didn't care about things like manicures, or getting her hair colored like Lexi's mom did, but maybe that stuff was really important to Lana.

"I think that's a great idea," my dad agreed. "You've

all been working really hard with your bride and brides-maid duties and could use some pampering."

Cassie looked pleased that my dad approved of it. "Awesome. I can stop in there and get a pamphlet that lists all the services. Maybe we could go on Saturday, the day before the wedding."

Because it was a small wedding—only twenty people—my dad and Lana had decided to have it on a Sunday afternoon, with the ceremony at a really nice Italian restaurant called Cara Mia, followed by a small reception there.

"That sounds great," Lana said. "That way we'll be nice and relaxed." She reached over and pushed some hair off of Cassie's face. "You always have good ideas, Cass, but this one beats them all." She turned to us. "What do you girls think? You up for being pampered?"

"Totally," Kayley said.

"I don't know what 'pampered' means, but I think my answer is yes!" Sammi cried, and we all laughed.

Lana looked at me. "Avery, what about you? You don't look too convinced."

Cassie's smile disappeared as she waited for my response.

"Oh. No, I think a spa day is a great idea. . . ."

Her regular smug smile returned.

"Great," Lana said.

"It's just . . ." I shook my head. "Never mind."

"What is it, honey?" Dad asked.

I shook my head again. "Nothing. The more I think about it, it's probably a dumb idea I have."

"There are no dumb ideas around here," Lana said gently. Cassie, however, did not look convinced about that.

I felt myself turn red. "It's just that one night when Lexi was sleeping over, we were looking online for do-it-yourself facial masks, and we found this site that told you how to do an at-home spa night."

"That sounds interesting," my dad said.

"What was neat about it was that all the recipes used stuff you could find in your kitchen or at the grocery store, so not only was it cheap, but it was healthy, too," I went on.

"Ooh—I love that!" Lana exclaimed. "I always

get nervous about not knowing what chemicals are in cleansers and things like that."

Cassie looked like this was the most disgusting thing she had ever heard.

"Plus, it sounds like more of an opportunity for you guys to bond than being at a spa," said my dad.

"That's a good point," Lana agreed.

"I think Avery's idea is wonderful," Cassie said in a sickly sweet voice. "And something that would be a ton of fun to do on a *regular* Saturday night—you know, a *non*-special-occasion one."

"Cassie's right," I said nervously. *Why* had I brought this up?! All the work I had done to make her like me, and now I was back to square one! "It's not something you do before an important event. Like a wedding."

"To me, that sounds like the best time to do it," Lana said. She turned to my dad. "What do you think, sweetheart? Do you think you can find some way to amuse yourself while we have a Girls' Night In a week from Saturday?"

"Nothing would make me happier," he said, giving me a big smile.

I tried to smile back, but I had a feeling it looked pretty wobbly. Especially when I saw Cassie glaring at me out of the corner of my eye.

Usually when I came up with something that people thought was a great idea, it made me feel good about myself.

This time I couldn't have felt more awful.

Until I found out that I could.

I didn't check my phone until I got home that night, and when I did, there were a bunch of texts from Lexi asking me where I was. It was only then that I realized I had totally spaced on our plans to meet at Painting Pals that night. I immediately texted her, but she ignored it. Just like she ignored the nine other ones I sent after that, as well as my five phone calls before I finally gave up and went to bed.

The next morning I tried again and received a response that said, THIS IS A TEXT LETTING YOU KNOW THAT I'M NOT SPEAKING TO YOU AT THE MOMENT.

Knowing she probably wouldn't answer the phone

if I tried to call again, I hopped on my bike and rode two blocks over to her house.

"Lexi, I feel so awful," I panted when she answered the door. It had been a long time since I had ridden my bike.

"Well, you should," she replied with a glare.

"It's just that I was so focused on the charm bracelet thing, and then my dad called and invited me to dinner, and then when I was there, this spa night idea came up, and then—"

"I get it. You're super busy with your new family," she snapped.

"It's just that—"

"It's just that ever since the BBs showed up, you spend all your time trying to impress them, without remembering the people who have stuck by you before you even knew they existed!" she cried.

I shrank back. I had never seen Lexi so mad. But the thing was—she was right. I *had* been spending all my time focused on the BBs and trying to get them to like me.

"You're right," I said quietly. "I have been. Which

is totally stupid, because even if they never do like me, it doesn't matter because I already have a sister—you."

"Yeah, well, you sure haven't been treating me like one lately," she grumbled.

"I know that. And I'm really, really sorry. But I promise from now on things are going to be different. Do you think you can forgive me?"

She thought about it. "I *guess*," she finally said.

I smiled, and after a second she smiled back.

"Thank you," I said as I hugged her hard.

"You're welcome," she replied. "Now, what's all this about a spa night?" she asked as we let go.

I shook my head. "Oh, it's nothing," I lied.

"Um, hello? Yes, it is. Tell me," she ordered.

"No. I don't want to talk about them. I want to hear about last night. Who was there?"

She waved her hand. "It was fine. Kind of boring, actually. Now tell me."

"But you just said I spend too much time talking about them!"

"Well, it's not like you have to stop talking about them *completely*. All I'm saying is that you can't forget the people who have been there for you since the beginning."

I nodded. "I know. And I haven't. And I won't."

"Good." She grabbed my hand and pulled me inside. "Now tell me everything!"

"Look at it this way—things could be worse," Lexi said the next afternoon as she lay on my bed with her head almost touching the floor, while I halfheartedly surfed the web for DIY home spa recipes. After I got home from Lexi's yesterday, I texted Cassie to ask if there was anything special she wanted me to look for recipewise—like, say, a salt scrub or a sugar scrub, but she didn't reply. And then I sent her another text asking if she had dry hair or oily hair, because there were different masks for specific types of hair, and I wanted to find one she liked, but she didn't respond to that, either. And then I sent her *another* text asking her what color nail polish she thought we should all wear, because I could ride my bike into town and go to the pharmacy there and take some photos and send them to her and she could choose. No answer to that, either. The whole thing made me look pathetic, but I couldn't help it. The more I thought about it, the more I could understand why she was so mad. Here she had brought up an idea that everyone loved, and then I had to mess it up by trying to outdo her. If someone did that to me, I'd be mad too. But the thing was, I *wasn't* trying to outdo her. I didn't even want to tell Lana what I was thinking about. I just happened to have what Mom called an "expressive" face, which made it so that I couldn't hide anything on it. According to her, people with expressive faces were really bad at poker, but I didn't care about that because I had no idea how to play it.

I looked up from the computer. "Really? How could they be worse?" I asked doubtfully.

Lexi raised herself up into a sitting position. "I don't know exactly," she confessed, "but don't people always say that to make someone feel better?"

I sighed. "I guess so."

She grabbed her head. "Uh-oh. Head rush." She grabbed my new *Seventeen* that had just come in the mail that afternoon. "Hey, do you think I should get my hair cut like her?" she asked, pointing at the model with the very short pixie cut.

I loved Lexi, but she got sidetracked *really* easily. "No," I replied.

"You're probably right," she agreed. "Because if I did—"

"You'd freak out every single time you got a zit and you'd make it worse with all the ways you'd try and get rid of it."

She gasped. "That's *exactly* what I was going to say! How'd you know that?"

"Um, maybe because I'm your best friend?"

"Right."

I got up and started organizing my jewelry. When I was nervous, that always made me feel better. Needless to say, it was something I had been doing a lot of since this whole wedding thing.

Lexi started going through my closet. "Remember the shorts incident with Linley Anderson in fifth grade?"

I wrinkled my nose. "Of course. How could I forget that?" Linley was the most popular girl in our grade and literally walked around with her nose stuck up in the air. I bet her neck really hurt. I had hated her ever since she completely embarrassed Lexi by stealing her regular clothes out of her locker during gym class, which meant that she had to walk to the office in her shorts, which she was totally embarrassed to do because they were short-shorts and she hated her thighs. (I personally loved her thighs because, unlike mine, which looked like undercooked pieces of spaghetti, hers were really strong.)

"And remember when I used to cry about how I couldn't understand why she hated me, and tried to come up with a list of things I could do differently to make her like me, and you told me I was being insane?"

"Yeah. Because you *were*." My experience had been that when it came to MPGs (mean popular girls), the idea of logic didn't apply. Lexi had never done anything but be nice to Linley—a lot nicer than I had been—and while they had never exactly been friends, they got along well enough to say hi to each other in the hall and stuff like that. Until one day Linley completely turned on her. For no reason.

"And remember when we were downstairs in the kitchen, and I was crying as we ate that bag of Reese's peanut butter cups that your mom had hidden on the top shelf, where she thought we didn't know about it, but we did because everyone knows that the top shelf of a pantry is always the first place to look for something that someone is trying to hide?"

"Yup." I didn't add *How could I forget?* but the truth was I couldn't forget, because when she's super upset, Lexi is an ugly crier.

"And remember your mom came home right then?"

"Uh-huh." After that the Reese's hiding place changed. To the top of her closet, which is the second place people look when trying to find something that's hidden.

"Do you remember what she said to me?"

"Not really," I admitted. Mostly because I had been too worried about the different punishments I could get for eating the Reese's.

"She said that not everyone is going to like you, but if you're lucky, you'll find a few people who love you all of the time, even if they don't like you sometimes," she said. "And she said the reason they're going to love you is because they love lots of different things about you, even the things you yourself don't like, so it's a waste of time to try and change who you are."

I nodded. It was coming back to me. "Wow. My mom's really smart," I said, surprised.

"Totally," Lexi agreed. "So the good news is—see, there *is* good news, it just took me a while to find it— the good news is that you already have me in that love category. Which is huge, if I do say so myself. So if that's the case, why bother trying to change just so Cassie likes you? You didn't do anything wrong. You came up with a great idea—that's what you do! You come up with great ideas all the time! That's a *good* thing."

She wasn't wrong. I did come up with good ideas on a semiregular basis.

"And if Cassie doesn't like it, that's her problem," she went on. "But don't stop doing it."

Ten

The next week was crazy busy. On Monday, Lana took us shoe shopping for shoes for our bridesmaid dresses. (Cassie and Kayley got high heels, while Sammi and I got flats. I had trouble walking in heels on a normal day, let alone one when I was going to be super nervous.) And then on Tuesday we had to go back to the scene of the (Frappuccino) crime and make sure our dresses fit okay once they had been altered. (Lana also took us for haircuts (really just trims, because she warned us that right before a wedding was *not* the time to experiment with a new style, something she knew from experience, having chopped all her hair off into a pixie cut before her sister's wedding when she was twenty-one).

The more time I spent with them, the more comfortable I felt. Well, with everyone but Cassie. While she wasn't downright mean to me, she wasn't warm, either. Still, I took Lexi's advice (or rather, my mom's advice) and just kept being myself—even to the point of singing out loud when Beyoncé came on while we were in the car going to the mall to pick up our dresses, which was something I *always* did because Beyoncé was my complete favorite singer. The thing was, I had a horrible voice. Like, even my *mom* said I had a horrible voice, and moms were supposed to love everything about you. Everyone tried to keep a straight face, but I could see that it was tough. When the song was over, I looked at them and said, "I'm thinking of trying out for *The Voice*—what do you think?" I tried to keep a straight face, but I couldn't, and once they realized that I was kidding, they all burst out laughing. After that I felt much better, not to mention much closer to all of them. It was kind of like the beginning of a private joke.

Cassie wasn't with us then, though. Which was probably why I felt comfortable enough to sing. When Lana drove up and I came out of the house and got into the car and noticed she wasn't there and asked about it, I saw Kayley and Sammi exchange a glance. "She's . . . not feeling all that well today," said Lana.

"Oh," I said. "Well, I hope she's better soon."

"She'll be fine," Lana said.

It was hard to miss the way Kayley raised her eyebrows at that.

"She's not sick," Kayley whispered to me later as Lana looked for some special slip thing to wear under her wedding dress.

I looked up from a silk nightgown with the feathered neckline I was stroking, wondering how someone could sleep in it without it tickling her nose and making her sneeze all night. "She's not?"

She shook her head. "No. She's upset about our dad."

I let the nightgown fall. I knew that their dad was back in California, but this was the first anyone had ever mentioned him. "Oh. Sorry to hear that." I tried to make it sound like I wasn't dying to hear more. Which

I totally was. When she didn't say any more, I couldn't help myself. "So . . . why is she upset?"

Kayley glanced over to where Lana was now talking to the saleslady. "She's upset because she called him the other day to ask if she could come live with him, and he said no."

WHAT?! That was *huge*! "Why'd she do that?" I asked, shocked.

"She said she wants to live with people who want her," she replied.

"Why would she say *that*?" By this point I wasn't even trying to hide my surprise about the whole thing.

"She'd totally deny it, but I think she's worried that you're going to be everyone's favorite."

It was a good thing I wasn't chewing gum, because if I was, it would've fallen out because my mouth was stuck in the shape of a big O. "Okay, that's completely nuts," I said once I managed to get it closed. "Why would she ever think *that*?"

She shrugged. "Lots of reasons, I guess. The way that Mom and Matt thought your idea for the spa night at home was so awesome, and the fact that our mom thinks you're really smart and funny and nice, and she loves how sweet you've been to Sammi. And how your dad was bragging about how creative you are."

I couldn't believe it. Not just the things that everyone was saying about me, but the fact that I'd want to move too if I were Cassie. "That makes me sound so . . . ," I said, confused.

"So what?" she asked.

I shrugged. "I don't know. So . . . much better than I am."

She laughed. "What are you talking about? It's all true."

I wanted to keep telling her she was wrong, but I was afraid that would make me look like I was just fishing for more compliments. "Wow. That's too bad about your dad," I said instead. "That would really hurt to hear something like that." I couldn't even imagine. While my dad obviously hadn't paid all that much attention to me in the past, I had liked to believe that if I had asked him if I could come live with him, he would've said yes.

Kayley shrugged. "Yeah, it is too bad, but I don't know why she acted like it was some big surprise."

"It wasn't?"

She shook her head. "No way. Ever since he married our stepmonster and they had the twins, he pretty much acts like we don't exist."

Whoa. I had had no idea about any of this. Probably because those are the kinds of things you only tell your close friends. I had known that their dad was remarried and had kids, but not the rest of it.

"How often do you guys see him?"

"It was supposed to be every other weekend, but then he told our mom that he didn't have time for that, so now it's two weeks in the summer. But last time he and the stepmonster went away to France for a week and left us with the nanny."

Wow. That sounded like something out of a movie.

"I'm really sorry, Kayley," I said. "That just ... sucks."

"Yeah. It does," she agreed. "That's why we were so psyched when your dad asked our mom to marry him. It'll be nice to have a dad who actually pays attention to us. You've been really lucky to have him."

After hearing what I just heard, I realized I was. "Yeah. I am," I said quietly, looking down at the floor.

"What's the matter?" she asked.

I looked up. "Nothing. I mean, all this time I thought you guys had, like, the perfect lives," I confessed.

She laughed so hard she actually snorted. And not a dainty little snort, which was the kind of snort I thought would come out of her, but a . . . messy snort. Which I loved, because it made her so not perfect. "As if! If anyone's got the perfect life, it's *you*."

Now it was my turn to laugh. "Yeah right."

We shared a smile.

"Can I tell you something?" I blurted out.

"Sure."

"The first time I had breakfast with you guys? I changed my outfit *seven* times," I confessed. Just saying that aloud made my shoulders feel twenty pounds lighter.

"I changed mine twice," she admitted. "And I probably would've a third time, but we were already late."

We laughed. A real laugh. Like the kind I had with Lexi.

"And just so you know, before this I barely had a relationship with my dad," I confessed.

Kayley looked shocked. "Seriously?"

I nodded. "Yeah. It was bad. I only saw him a few times a year, and he barely returned my e-mails."

"Wow. I never would have guessed that. You guys are so close now," she said wistfully.

I shrugged. "We're getting there. Time takes time, though."

"Huh. I like that. It's catchy."

"Isn't it? I learned it from him."

We shared another smile.

"I wish there was something I could do to make things better with Cassie," I sighed.

"Honestly, I wouldn't worry about it," she replied. "She'll come around eventually."

That was good to know.

"And if she doesn't, two out of three of us isn't so bad," she added with a smile.

Kayley might have told me to leave things alone with Cassie, but I just couldn't. I was one of those people who couldn't stand to have people mad at me, or think things about me that weren't true, and in this case, both of those things were happening.

My mom had once told me that sometimes when you were frustrated, it helped to write things and not send them. That way you blew off some steam, but you didn't have to worry about getting in trouble with your words. So after dinner, as my mom talked back to the TV while we watched *The Bachelorette* (she was always telling people that we watched it because *I* liked it, but really it was because of her), I picked up my phone and I drafted a text:

hey cassie. missed seeing you today. wanted to know if we could hang out this week. just the 2 of us. need to talk to you.

I had to admit, it made me feel better to write it, even if I wasn't sending it. It made me feel so good, in fact, that as I erased it, I drafted another one.

i'd say hope you're feeling better, but i heard you're not really sick. well, i am—of all this stuff between us. can we please get together and talk it out?

That made me feel even better. Especially the "well, i am" sentence, on account of the fact that it was really clever, if I did say so myself. There was something to this stuff, I thought as I erased that one.

how long exactly do you plan on being such a jerk to me?

Okay, that was pushing it. I couldn't send a text like that and expect a good response.

But then I did.

Because as I was backspacing and deleting it, my finger slipped (that's what I got for not washing my hands after eating greasy french fries) and pushed the send button. So the text read, how long exactly do you plan on being such a jerk.

"OH MY GOD!" I screamed as the words showed up on the screen. Not only did I sound like a horrible person, but I looked stupid because it didn't have any punctuation.

"What happened?! What's the matter?!" Mom asked, panicked. I heard her, but I didn't see her due to the fact that my eyes were screwed closed tight because I was trying to do that deep-breathing thing she had taught me that she did in yoga that was supposed to relax you. Unfortunately, it wasn't doing that for me. All it was doing was making it harder to breathe because I was gasping for air.

Eyes still closed, I felt around blindly for the phone and grabbed it and threw it in the direction of her voice.

"*Ow*," she said. "Sweetheart, watch where you aim."

I opened my eyes to see her rubbing her chest as she looked at the phone. Whoops. Her eyes widened as she read the text. "Why would you send this?!"

"I didn't!" I cried. "What I mean is that I didn't *mean* to send it! I was trying to take your advice!"

"When did I give you advice to accuse someone of being a jerk?" she asked. She looked at the phone more closely. "And not even use punctuation with it, to boot?"

I rolled my eyes. That's what you got for having an English professor for a mother. "No—the advice you gave me to write things out and then get rid of them because just writing them would make me feel better."

"Oh. Right. Yeah, that always works for me," she said. "But you sent it."

For someone who had gone to school for so many years, sometimes my mom could be pretty slow. "I sent it by *mistake*," I explained. "My finger slipped."

"Oh. *Oh*," she said, finally getting it. "Oh, this is not good," she said as she shook her head.

"THAT PART I KNOW!" I cried. "What I need to know is how to fix it!"

"Oh. Well, that's easy," she said.

"How?"

"Just recall the text before she reads it."

"You can't do that," I sighed. Not only did my mom like to point out the obvious, but she had zero understanding of how technology worked. She still sent *letters* to people.

"You can't? I feel like I've done that before. . . ." She stared at the phone. "Hold on—she texted back."

"What does it say?!" I demanded, lunging for the phone.

"It says 'excuse me' in all caps with four exclamation points."

Uh-oh. Caps were not good. And they were *especially* not good now. I snatched the phone out of her hand. "What should I text back?"

"Nothing," Mom replied. "You should stop this texting nonsense and call her and talk to her."

I looked at her like she had just suggested I strip down naked and get on the roof and sing Beyoncé's

"Single Ladies (Put a Ring on It)," which was my go-to karaoke song.

"I know I've said this before, but while all this technology is supposed to help people connect, it also allows them not to have to take responsibility for themselves and show up and have difficult conversations and—"

"Mom. Please. Not the technology lecture now." I could pretty much recite it by heart. "Even if I did call her, what would I say?"

"The truth. That you'd like to talk things out once and for all so that you can start having a real relationship, seeing that within a week you're going to be family."

At that, I literally crawled under the patchwork quilt that was on the couch with me. I popped my head out. "Isn't there something else I could say?"

"Not if you want to tell the truth."

I sighed. "Let me guess: I should just be the bigger person and do this."

"You got it," she replied.

I pulled the blanket over my head again.

* * *

It wasn't the lecture about how this kind of stuff was "character-building" and that in the long run I'd end up being grateful for the opportunity to "leave my comfort zone" so that I could "stretch and grow" that made me take Mom's advice and finally call Cassie. It was the Ben & Jerry's Chunky Monkey ice cream that she let me get before doing it.

"Hi . . . Cassie?" I said when she answered.

"Yeah?" she said icily.

"It's, uh, Avery."

"Yeah?" she replied just as icily.

"*Cassie,*" I heard Lana warn in the distance. It made me feel better to know she was standing over Cassie like Mom was standing over me.

"Obviously, I didn't mean to send that text," I said.

"Yeah, well, you did."

I sighed. So much for Mom's prediction that this call was going to go much better than I thought it would. "Do you think we can get together so that I can apologize in person?"

"*Yes. You can,*" I heard Lana whisper. Wow. Either

I talked really loud or she was really close to the phone.

"Fine," Cassie said.

We decided to meet at Javalicious at three o'clock the next afternoon, because Lana had errands to do around there anyway. Cassie was already there when I got there, thumbing through a copy of *Us Weekly*.

I walked up behind her. "I love the Stars—They're Just Like Us! section," I said over her shoulder. "Especially the pictures where they're, like, taking out the garbage and stuff like that."

She turned and gave me a look as if I had said, *I like to eat garbage*.

"It just makes them so . . . normal," I said nervously.

She closed the magazine. "Yeah. Whatever."

I sighed. "I'm going to get a Chillsie. Do you want one?"

"Nope," she said, and went back to her magazine. This was going well so far. "Okay. I'll be right back."

As I stood in line, I kept stealing looks at her out of the corner of my eye, hoping to see her in a different light. Meaning one where I had sympathy for her for what Kayley had told me, instead of seeing her for what she looked like at that moment: a stuck-up princess who judged everyone and everything and found them to come up short.

"So . . . that text," I began, staring down at my drink once I had joined her back at the table. "It was a mistake."

"Yeah. *I'll* say," she replied. I sighed. If this was how the conversation was starting, I could only imagine how it was going to end. *Be the bigger person . . . be the bigger person*, I said to myself as I took a deep breath. "What I *mean* is that what I was trying to say was that I was sick of us fighting and wanted to know if we could talk this out once and for all."

"Talk what out?" she asked innocently. "We don't fight."

My eyes narrowed. She wasn't going to make this easy. And I was sick of it. No more beating around the bush. "You're right. We don't," I agreed.

A small smirk started to bloom on her face.

"Instead you just say all these things to me that maybe technically aren't insults, but actually are."

Robin Palmer

The smirk deflated. "Ex*cuse* me?"

"Yeah. Like that," I went on, "talking to me like you're the queen and I'm . . . I don't know . . . your chambermaid!" *Chambermaid?* I wasn't sure what had come over me, but whatever it was had obviously downed a Red Bull, judging by how revved up I was. "From the very beginning I've gone out of my way to be nice to you. I've sucked it up, I've been the bigger person, I've—"

She rolled her eyes. "Okay, obviously someone needs a time-out right now—"

"I do not!" I cried, sounding just like a kid who did need a time-out.

From the way a bunch of people turned to look at me, it was obvious that had also come out *a lot* louder than I meant it to. I shrank down in my chair, hoping the floor would open and swallow me up. "See? Even when you're not technically embarrassing me, you still figure out a way to embarrass me!" I hissed. I knew I sounded like a crazy person, but I couldn't help it. This was what I did. Because I was so afraid of there being weirdness between me and other people if I told them how I really felt, I instead let things build up and build

♥ 192 ♥

up until I exploded. It wasn't pretty, and as Mom liked to remind me, it wasn't fair to them.

From the look on Cassie's face, I *was* a crazy person. "Are you *done* now?"

I stared at her. She just didn't get it. Why was I even wasting my time? Yes. I was done. Big-time. So what if I hated my stepsister? Lots of people did. That was the entire basis of fairy tales! "No. I'm not," was what came out of my mouth instead. Oh no. "I just need to say one last thing." Did I really?

"What's that?"

"I need to say . . . that I know you weren't sick yesterday."

Her *I just sucked on a lemon* face was replaced by surprise.

"And that . . . I'm sorry about your dad, and how he said you couldn't come live with him."

The surprise turned to something in the neighborhood of fear. "How do you know about that?" she whispered.

"It doesn't matter," I replied. The last thing I needed was to get Kayley mad at me. "But I want to say that

I'm sure it really, really sucks to be told something like that. And while I can't imagine it *exactly*, until recently I didn't get along all that well with my dad."

"You didn't?" She seemed genuinely surprised by this.

"Well, it wasn't like we had fights or anything like that," I said. "We would have had to actually *talk* in order to do that."

She looked confused.

"My dad's said more to me in the last few weeks than he has in probably my entire life," I went on. "Before now we barely ever saw each other, let alone talked."

"I didn't know that," she said softly. "You guys seem so close."

I laughed. "Hardly." I sighed. "Do you know what it feels like to send your own father an e-mail telling him about your life and he doesn't even bother replying?"

"Yeah. I do," she said, angry. But I could tell this time the anger wasn't directed toward me. It was toward him.

Now it was my turn to be surprised. "It seems like we finally have something in common, I guess."

She looked at me. This time there was no lemon sucking. This time I saw a girl who looked just as sad as I had felt all those years when it came to my dad. Someone who wondered what she had done wrong to make one of the two people who were supposed to love her no matter what not even want to bother talking to her.

"I'm *really* sorry, Cassie," I said.

"Thanks," she said softly. "I am too."

"Look, I know being older, and coming from California, you must think I'm a total dork, but—"

"No, I don't. I actually think you're really cool," she admitted. "Which is probably why I've been such a jerk to you."

Wait a minute—what?

"When I saw how great my mom thought you were, I started to get worried that soon enough I'd have two parents who didn't care about me anymore."

Whoa. That made total sense. Not that that would happen, but that she'd *worry* that would happen.

Because that's exactly what I would think if I was her. Maybe we had more in common than I thought.

"I get it," I said.

"You do?"

I nodded. "Yeah. And I'm sorry you had to walk around feeling like that."

She gave a shy smile. "And I'm sorry that you had to walk around with me being such a jerk to you."

"Yeah. It kind of sucked. Like, *a lot*," I replied.

She flinched, which made me feel bad, but if I was sitting here going on about honesty, I kind of had to do it myself, too.

"I bet it did," she said softly. "I really am sorry."

"It's okay," I said. That wasn't a lie. I really did mean it.

"Do you think we can start over?" she asked.

I nodded. "Yeah. We can."

Eleven

♥

After Cassie and I smoothed things over, the Girls' Night In went from something I was dreading to something I couldn't wait for. I probably went a bit overboard with the planning (me and Mom stayed up until midnight the night before making *seven* different kinds of salt scrubs!), but it was hard not to when so many great things came up when you searched for "home spa recipes" on Pinterest.

"Well, if you ever decide to stop being a jewelry designer," Mom said as she helped me carry everything up the front walk of my dad's house the next evening, "you definitely have a career making beauty products." She took the top off a strawberry honey facial mask and dipped her finger in it.

"Mom, you need to stop eating all of it!" I cried.

"I know, I know. It's just so *good*," she said as she took another fingerful. "Not to mention good for you."

I was surprised she hadn't eaten the coffee grounds body scrub yet.

Lana had already opened the door and was waiting for us with a smile. "Well, hello there." She looked at all our bags. "Wow. This looks more like a Girls' *Month* In."

"I went a little overboard," I confessed.

She turned to Mom. "Monica, I meant to do this earlier, but I've been so crazed. Would you like to join us?"

Mom shook her head. "Thanks, but I can't. I actually have . . . a date." You could tell by the way she moved her mouth up and down that she wasn't used to saying those words. Mom hated dating. She said that it was worse than getting her eyebrows waxed, and she *hated* getting her eyebrows waxed.

"Really? How great!" Lana exclaimed. She shook

her head. "Boy, was I happy once I got engaged, just to know that I wouldn't have to date again. I was a horrible dater."

"So is Mom!" I said excitedly. "Once, there was this guy named Ted and—"

Mom put her hand on my arm. "Avery, I'm sure Lana is way too busy to hear that story," she said, cutting me off.

The only reason I was bringing it up was because I thought it was great that they had something in common. That and the fact that it was a really good story because it was about how this guy Ted referred to himself as "Ted" the whole night instead of using "I." And that wasn't even the good part. The good part was that he brought his *cat* with him to dinner, in a carrier that looked like a house, and got all huffy when the hostess wouldn't let him bring it into the restaurant.

"Okay," I said, and shrugged.

"Well, I hope you guys have a terrific time," Mom said as she leaned in to kiss me on the cheek. She turned to Lana. "I'll be back in the morning to get her."

"Oh, I can drop her off," Lana said.

"Don't be silly," Mom replied. "You have enough to do the day of your wedding without driving an hour out of your way."

"Okay," Lana said, sounding a little disappointed.

Mom patted her on the shoulder. "Stop being Superwoman and just be the bride."

Lana looked hurt.

"I'm *joking*," Mom said.

Lana looked confused for a second and then smiled. "Oh. Got it."

Mom and I had talked about how Lana was always going a million miles a minute and trying to make sure everyone was taken care of and happy. She also wasn't a big joker, which, for people like me and Mom, made things a little awkward because we liked to joke a lot.

I had to say it made me feel good how impressed everyone seemed to be not just with everything I'd brought, but with how I had made spa goodies that incorporated things they liked.

"Mmm . . . bananas are my FAVORITE!" Sammi yelled as she took a whiff of the body lotion I had made for her. In addition to whipped bananas, it also had almond and coconut oils, which made it extra yummy. She stuck a finger in it and brought it to her mouth. "Wait—can I eat it too?"

I nodded. "If you want."

She tasted it. "It's DELICIOUS!" she exclaimed, and we all laughed. I loved how Sammi got excited about everything. I couldn't wait to hang out with her even more with Lexi.

I held out a container to Kayley. "And this one is for you."

She opened it and sniffed it. "Lemon and peppermint?" she guessed.

I nodded. "Yeah. It's a foot scrub. I remembered you mentioning that your feet were all rough from walking around outside without shoes. And I know peppermint is your favorite flavor of gum, because you bought the multipack of Orbit when we were at the mall last week."

She smiled. "You have a good memory." She reached over and hugged me. "Thanks."

She had never hugged me before. In fact, I knew from eavesdropping once when Lana was on the phone with her best friend, Beth, that Kayley had this thing where she didn't like to be touched. Just like she had to check that the lights were off in her room every time they left the house. So the hug felt extra special. I hugged back. "You're welcome." I turned to Cassie. "I saw on Facebook how you posted that article about the nail art, so I thought this would be neat," I said as I took out a hand scrub made of avocado and honey, as well as a bunch of different pastel nail polishes.

Cassie smiled. The first real smile I had seen on her face, I realized. "Those are great colors. Thanks."

Sammi peered at the scrub. "Can we eat this one too?"

"Sure," I laughed.

Lana picked it up. "How about we save this for dessert?" she asked as she winked at me. "This was so thoughtful of you, Avery," she said.

I shrugged. "It wasn't that big of a deal. Plus, I like doing this stuff. It's like the crafting version of cooking." That was a bit of a lie; doing all the research and then gathering all the ingredients had actually been super time-consuming, but their reactions had made it worth it. I took out a tube. "And this one is for you,"

I said as I handed it to Lana. "I heard you say that this weather was making your hair really dry, so I went to the spa and got this."

Lana looked at the tube. This one wasn't all natural like the other ones, but the lady who owned the place had sworn that it made your hair as soft as velvet. "Avery, you shouldn't have spent your money on this."

"Oh, I didn't," I replied.

Lana looked alarmed.

"I didn't *steal* it or anything like that," I assured her. "I traded it for a bracelet I made." Which was a good thing, because the hair mask was expensive. Like, twenty bucks.

She looked impressed. "Wow. It must have been a nice bracelet." She hugged me. "Thank you. We really appreciate this. Don't we, girls?"

They all nodded.

"Now let's get this party started," she said with a smile.

The night was awesome. I had such a good time that I almost felt guilty. Especially when I texted Mom at eight thirty to ask how her date was going and she told me she was already home in bed with Netflix on. At nine o'clock we all put facial masks on, and Lana also put her hair mask on, wrapping her hair up in a towel as it soaked in.

"You should try it too," I said to Cassie. "They say that it also helps to make wavy hair straighter." I knew that she was already planning on using the straightening iron on her hair the next day, so maybe this would take away the need for that.

"Cool," she said as she picked up the tube and walked toward the bathroom. She came out with her hair up in a towel like Lana.

After that we decided to present Lana with her something new/old/blue gifts. She loved the blue turtle that Sammi had picked out, and when we gave her the charm bracelet, she actually started crying. (Not the best thing to do when you have a facial mask on, because it makes the mask get all goopy and fall off your face in big drops onto your clothes.)

"I don't know what to say," she said as she dabbed at her eyes with a tissue. "This might be the most thoughtful gift I've ever gotten."

"It was all Avery's idea," Cassie said.

I looked at her, surprised. Really? She was going to give me credit for this?

"It was," she insisted.

"Well, it's very creative," Lana said.

I felt my face turn red. "Thanks," I mumbled. You would've thought that I'd be happy to have her acknowledge the fact that I came up with it, but it was super awkward. Now that we weren't fighting anymore, I wanted us to be seen as a team.

"Sammi, honey, what's the matter?" Lana said. "You keep swiping at your face."

"This stuff is making it really itchy," she whined as she scratched some off.

Kayley cringed as she started patting her own face. "Mine too."

I realized that the warmth I had been feeling on my face wasn't just from embarrassment, but from the mask as well.

Cassie grabbed a napkin and started swiping at her cheeks. "What did you put in this thing?" she demanded.

"I just followed the recipe!" I said as I started scratching at my own. They weren't just warm now—they were stinging.

Lana ran into the kitchen and came back with a roll of paper towels. "Here. Everyone wipe it off," she ordered as she took her own mask off.

Once I saw her skin, I gasped.

"What is it?!" she asked, panicked.

"Your skin . . . it's kind of red," I replied nervously.

"Kind of red?!" Cassie cried. "It's like a giant sunburn with tomato juice squeezed on top of it!"

I don't know if I would have gone as far as the tomato juice, but it did look like a sunburn. Like the kind you'd have if you were, I don't know, very close to the sun.

Lana took a deep breath. "Avery. What exactly was in that recipe?" She was trying to sound calm, but I could hear the panic seeping through.

I finished wiping off the mask and grabbed my cell phone. "It's right here," I said. I was on the verge of tears by now. "It's just eggs and honey and avocado and a little bit of apple cider vinegar—"

Lana grabbed my phone and looked at the screen.

"The recipe calls for apple *cider*—not apple cider *vinegar*." She threw the phone on the couch in frustration.

"Uh-oh," I mumbled. "It was the last one I made last night. . . . I was already so tired . . . ," I sputtered. "I'm so sorry."

"Vinegar?! On our *faces*?!" Cassie cried. "You might as well have put acid in it!"

"I said I was sorry!" I cried. My eyes were stinging, but it wasn't from the mask. It was from the tears that were streaming down my face. I was so freaked out I wasn't even trying to hide them. I turned to Lana. "I didn't mean it."

"I know you didn't mean it, but maybe next time you'll be more careful when reading directions," she snapped, while trying to calm down Sammi, who by now was also crying and demanding to know if her skin was going to be scarred for life.

I picked up my phone and opened up Google. "Maybe I can find something about what to do when you put apple cider vinegar on your face." I scrolled down the screen. "Wait a minute—this says that it's actually good for your skin."

"It's probably the reaction it's having with the other ingredients that's causing the stinging," Kayley said.

If anyone would know, she would. Cassie had mentioned to me the other day that Kayley had won first prize at the school science fair last year but didn't like to talk about it because she thought it made her look like a geek. If I had won it, I wouldn't stop talking about it. I thought it was really cool when girls were good at science. Unfortunately, that was never going to happen to me because I was not one of those girls who fell into that category.

"Well, whatever it is, the sting is going away a bit," Lana said. She picked up a mirror. "And the redness is going down too." She looked at us. "How about everyone else?"

"It's stinging less," Kayley said.

"Mine too," Sammi agreed.

Lana looked at Cassie. "Cass? What about yours?"

"I *guess* it's not *burning* as much," she admitted as she gently placed her hand on her cheek.

I stopped myself from rolling my eyes. Talk about a drama queen.

"Mine feels *a lot* better," I offered.

Love You Like a Sister

"I think we're all going to live," Lana said. "And I'll go get some of my moisturizer out of my bathroom. That should help calm things down more."

As she started toward the stairs, I put out my hand to stop her. "Lana, I'm really, really—"

"You're really sorry. I know that, Avery," she said.

I looked at the floor. Honestly, I would have felt better if she just went ahead and yelled at me.

I turned to see all three BBs glaring at me. "I didn't mean—"

"You didn't mean to do it," Cassie interrupted. "Yeah. You mentioned that."

"You're acting like I planned this!" I cried. Before I could say anything else—like how I had *thought* that we were now friends but I guess I had been wrong—there was a scream from the bathroom. We all looked at one another and rushed up the stairs.

wrong?!" Cassie said as we piled into Lana's bathroom to find her furiously scrubbing her head with a towel.

As she let the towel fall to the floor, we saw for ourselves.

"Your hair is *blue*!" Kayley shrieked.

It was. Like, *really* blue.

"I like it," Sammi piped up. "Mommy, can my hair be blue too?"

"Oh no. It must be from the mask," I gasped.

Cassie's eyes widened. "That means mine's going to be blue too!" she wailed. "We don't know that for sure," Lana said. Although she was trying to keep her voice calm, I could still hear some panic.

"Mommy, can it? Can my hair be blue too?" Sammi asked again.

Lana got her hair colored. Maybe something in the mask had had a reaction with the color, and that's why it had done that. But Cassie didn't color hers. So hers would be fine. A girl could dream, right?

Cassie tore off her towel and turned to us.

A girl could dream, but that didn't mean it was going to come true.

Hers was most definitely not fine. In fact, even more blue.

"Is it?" she asked anxiously.

"Is it what?" I asked, stalling.

"Blue!"

"Define 'blue,'" I replied. "Like, do you mean *navy* blue . . . because it's not that . . ."

She ran to the bathroom mirror and screamed. "WHAT HAVE YOU DONE TO US?!"

"Cassie, I swear I didn't know this was going to happen!" I cried. I turned to Lana, who looked like she had just been run over by a truck and then dragged a couple hundred miles by it. "I swear I didn't. The product must be defective—"

"I'll tell you who's defective. *You* are," Cassie shot back.

I felt like I had been slapped.

"Cassie—" Lana warned.

But she was on a roll. "You act all sweet and stuff, but that was just so you could then do *this*! You knew there was no way we could fix this by tomorrow!"

"I told you I didn't—"

She shook her head. "I can't believe I was stupid enough to believe you the other day and give you a real chance. I should have just stayed with my original idea of who you were from the beginning."

"And what was that?" I asked, my voice quivering. I knew that whatever the answer was would hurt, but I couldn't stop myself from asking.

"Some lonely girl with just one friend who thinks she's being all cool with her vintage stuff and DIY craft stuff but really is just a weirdo."

She might as well have taken the nail scissors that were sitting on top of the bathroom counter and stabbed me with them.

"CASSIE!" Lana yelled. "That's enough."

Cassie glared at me and stomped off to her room.

I turned to Kayley and Sammi. "Is that what you guys think of me?" I said quietly.

Kayley opened her mouth to say something but closed it again, before going toward Cassie's room. No surprise there.

"I think that her hair looks cool blue," Sammi said.

I smiled through my tears. "Yeah, it kind of does, doesn't it?"

She nodded and then looked torn. "I think I need to go and see if Cassie is okay."

I nodded back. "Yeah. Sure."

I slid down the wall and pulled myself into a ball. I knew that being able to make yourself disappear was something that happened only in books and movies, but I would've done anything to do that at that moment.

Lana came over and sat down with me. "Avery, I'm so sorry. She's just really upset at the moment—"

I pulled away from her. "What? It's true. I *am* weird."

"You are not," she said. "You're wonderfully creative." She patted my arm. "Don't worry, she'll calm down—"

"Yeah, and then something else will happen and she'll hate me again," I said. More tears streamed down my cheeks. "What's the use? No matter how long you and my dad are married, they're always going to be real sisters and I'll just be the step." I stood up and ran out of the room.

"Avery, wait!" Lana yelled. "Where are you going?"

I ran into my room and got my overnight bag and then ran downstairs and straight out the door. It was raining, but I didn't care. I needed to get as far away from all of them as possible.

Twelve

I was halfway down the block before I realized that I had forgotten my phone. "Seriously?" I sighed as I turned around and made my way back to the house.

When I walked in, I heard Lana's and Cassie's raised voices coming from upstairs. Luckily, I had left my phone in the living room, so I wouldn't have to see them. My plan was to call Mom and then go wait outside again. The only good thing about all this was that my dad wasn't here to see it. It was already mortifying enough without him.

I heard the front door open. "Lana?" a voice said.

And there he was.

Okay, then. There was officially *nothing* good about all this.

She must have called him and told him what had happened. I started hunting around for my phone in the living room. Maybe I could get out without him seeing me.

"Avery?" he said a second later. "What's going on?"

I turned around, still phoneless. "Hey, Dad," I said, miserable.

"Lana called me all frantic and wouldn't even tell me what was happening—just told me to come home right away. What happened?" He looked worried. And would probably be even more so once he found out that his daughter had ruined not just his wedding, but the lives of everyone involved.

Before I could open my mouth to explain, Lana ran down the stairs. "You're home," she said, relieved.

"Is someone going to tell me what happened?" he asked again. He had crossed over from worried to annoyed.

Lana sighed. "Well, it started with—"

"I've ruined everything," I interrupted. "That's what happened."

My dad looked at me, confused. "What are you talking about?" He looked at Lana. "And why is your hair *blue*?"

Before Lana could step in and try to sugarcoat things (how a person could sugarcoat blue hair would have been interesting to hear), her phone rang, and from the look of relief on her face, I could tell it was her hairdresser friend. After she'd walked into the kitchen, I told my dad everything. About the face mask, and the hair mask, and how Cassie hated me. "I knew this was a mistake," I said when I was done.

"What's a mistake?" he asked.

"Thinking that this could work out!" I cried.

"Who says it's not working out?" my dad said. "So you had a fight. Sisters fight."

Was he *insane*?! "This isn't a fight. Cassie *hates* me," I said. "And we're not sisters. We're *step*sisters. That's the problem." I shook my head. "You guys should just all go be a family. You don't need me to screw it up."

My dad started walking toward the stairs.

"What are you doing?" I asked, panicked.

"Calling the girls down here so that we can get this figured out once and for all."

I had once heard my mom tell her friend Maggie that one of the things that had driven her crazy about my dad was that he was such a . . . *guy* . . . in the way that he always wanted to get things fixed and figured out right away. Mom, on the other hand, liked to talk things out forever before actually doing anything about them. Which, according to her, was a very female thing to do.

"No! Don't!" I cried. "What I mean is . . . please just . . . don't."

He looked at me for a moment. "Would you rather I go up there and talk to them?"

I nodded, unable to trust my voice. I was afraid if I opened my mouth, I'd just start crying again.

"Okay," he said, nodding, as he came over and gave me a hug. "Avery, everything's going to be okay. I promise."

I shut my eyes, hoping he wouldn't let go. I didn't believe him, but I did feel pretty safe in his arms at the moment. Which was kind of a miracle, seeing that a month ago he could barely remember when my birthday was.

As he went up the stairs, I looked around for my phone. I probably couldn't get away with hiding in the garage anymore, but at least I could call Mom and have her come get me as soon as possible.

I finally found it—stuck between the couch cushions. As I went to get it, I noticed something gift wrapped in pink tissue paper peeking out from under the couch. I pulled it out and saw that the card on top of it said "Avery."

Surprised, I sat down on the couch and unwrapped it. It couldn't be a birthday gift—that was still six months away. I opened up the box to find a scrapbook. On the front cover it said "A Little Bit About Us . . ." in glitter. (Lots and lots of glitter, which led me to suspect that it was Sammi's doing.) Inside, the pages were filled with photos of Cassie, Kayley, and Sammi, along with postcards and pictures cut out from magazines, posted on pages that said "Things I Like" and "Things I Don't Like." It was like a combination of Facebook and Pinterest with a bit of Instagram thrown in.

Sammi's pages had pictures of gymnasts from the Olympics, as well as photos of her from tumbling class when she was little. And dogs. There were lots of dogs. (She was already pushing for the family to get a dog. And not just any dog, but a Bernese mountain dog. They were *huge*—when I Googled them, it said that they could weigh up to 120 pounds!) Sammi's pages were like her: bursting with color, and messy, and happy looking. It seemed weird to say that pages in a book could be happy, but that's how it felt to me.

Kayley's, on the other hand, were neat and orderly—just like her. The letters at the top were super straight, as if she had used a ruler underneath them. When I looked closer, I could see from the faint pencil line that had been erased that, actually, she had. Her pages had mostly pictures of dancers from the New York City Ballet. (One of her biggest freak-outs so far had been the fear that she wouldn't find a place she liked as much as her dance place in California, until I told her about one two towns over where a bunch of famous ballerinas had trained. That definitely earned me some points.) The feel of the pages wasn't so much happy looking as it was impressive. Impressive as in *Wow, that person must have spent an awful lot of time plotting out how to color-coordinate everything*. But in addition to that, there was something about seeing Kayley's pages that also made me feel sorry for her. They were *so* neat, *so* orderly, *so* perfect, that they didn't seem like a lot of fun. Not only that, but they seemed . . . *lonely*. I thought about the few times that I had been able to make her laugh, and what a sense of accomplishment I had felt. I guess because it didn't happen very often.

Cassie's pages were bold and sleek and sophisticated. Like looking at the pages of *Vogue* instead of *Seventeen*. There were pictures of Paris, and Rihanna, and fancy handbags, and high heels. The way everything was put together made it look like a magazine itself.

As I flipped the pages, I wondered why the girls were giving this to me. If anything, it made me feel even *more* separate and left out. Did I really need to be reminded that they were a trio and I was over in a corner by myself? It was like stabbing me with a knife and twisting it with a big smile. *Here's a gift . . . a gift that's going to make you feel even* more *like a loser.*

But then I turned the page again, to one that said "And Now . . . a Little Bit About YOU!" That was weird. There were pictures of me—ones starting from when I was a baby, which they must have gotten from Mom, all the way up to recent ones that had been taken by Lexi—with words cut out from magazines surrounding them. Words like "creative," "sassy," "one-of-a-kind." There was even one that said "razzmatazz" with a bunch of exclamation points after it. I wasn't sure what that meant, but then I remembered one day last week when Sammi was running around yelling it at the top of her lungs, so I figured she was responsible for that one. Especially because the way it was glued on wasn't the neatest. After all the pictures, I turned the page to find three pieces of lined notebook paper pasted onto the pages. Each was a letter that talked about the things they admired about me and how excited they were to have me as a sister.

Dazed, I shut the scrapbook. This had to be a mistake. Or maybe Lana had put them up to it. The whole thing was so . . . *nice.*

Just then my dad came down the stairs, followed by Lana—whose hair was still blue—and behind her, Kayley and Sammi.

My dad turned. "Cassie, get down here, please. *Now.*"

I heard the sound of heavy steps. The kind that said, *Fine, I'll come, but I'm doing this totally against my will and only because you're making me.*

When everyone was downstairs and seated in the living room, my dad began to pace. "Well, now seems like as good a time as any to have our first official meeting." He stopped midpace and gave us a look. "Lana filled me in on what happened and—more importantly—what was said by you girls."

I slunk down farther into the couch, to the point where I might as well have been lying down. Cassie's response was to cross her arms and stick her bottom lip out. Kayley looked like she was going to cry (I had noticed that that happened any time an adult didn't praise her). And Sammi? She was busy trying to get up into a headstand.

My dad seemed to be waiting for one of us to say something.

"Well, does anyone have anything to say?" he asked.

We all kept quiet.

Finally Sammi popped right side up and raised her hand.

"Yes, Sammi?" my dad said.

"That was the longest I've been able to stay up in a headstand," she replied. "It was four whole Mississippis."

From the way my dad's mouth twisted, I could tell he was trying not to laugh. "That's terrific, Sammi."

She nodded and put her head back down to get into another headstand.

"Anyone else have something to add?" he asked.

No one said anything.

"Okay. I'll talk, then." He started pacing again. "Blending a family together is never easy. I didn't expect this to happen without bumps in the road."

Bumps? In our case it was more like we had just driven off a *cliff*.

"Which is why communication is so important. I've had to learn the hard way what happens when you're not a good communicator," he said, looking at me, "and I don't want our family to suffer like that." He stopped pacing and said, "Avery, why don't you start?"

"Start with what?" I asked.

"Start with . . . what you'd like the girls to know. About, you know, what happened."

"I already said I was sorry!" I replied. "A bunch of times. Just like I already told Cassie and Lana that I have no idea why the hair mask made their hair turn blue!"

As I turned to Cassie, I caught her eyebrow going up. "You keep acting like I did it on purpose!"

"Avery . . . ," my dad warned.

"What? You said you wanted us to communicate. I'm communicating!"

"Yes, well, I'd like you to communicate a little less *loudly*, please."

I continued my slunking. I wasn't even sure if that was a word, but I liked it.

He turned to Cassie. "Cassie, would you like to share with us how you feel?"

"How do I feel?" she demanded. "Why don't we

start with how I *look*? Because how I *look* is totally ridic-ulous!"

My dad nodded. "I can understand how you might not feel that blue hair is all that attractive."

Cassie looked at him like he was nuts.

"But it's not the end of the world," he went on. He motioned to Lana. "Look at the bright side—you get to look like your mother!"

From the expression on Lana's face, that wasn't the best answer. In fact, from the glare she was giving my dad, that was a really *dumb* answer.

"Don't you need something blue for the wedding?" he asked.

She thought about it. "I guess that's one way of looking at it. . . ."

Sammi came down from her headstand. "But what about the blue turtle pin I got you?"

Lana smiled as she smoothed her hair back. "I guess I'll be lucky enough to have *two* blue things."

My dad exhaled. "Finally. Some progress." He turned to Cassie again. "Cassie, sometimes things happen that are out of our control. And we can either accept that and roll with it, or we can fight against it and be resentful toward other people."

Cassie continued to stare at the floor.

"Do you know what they say about resentment?" he asked.

"No," she mumbled.

"They say that resenting someone is like taking poison and thinking the other person is the one who will suffer."

"Huh. I like that," Kayley said.

"Thanks. Me too," he said with a smile, before putting his serious face back on. "Cassie, do you have anything to say about that?"

She looked up and opened her mouth to say something, but before she could, I raised my hand. "Can I say something?" I blurted out.

Instead of looking mad, she looked relieved that I had interrupted. I knew it was a risk, but if I didn't say what I was about to, I'd lose my nerve. I held up the scrapbook. "I just found this."

Cassie looked like she wished it was back under the couch.

Love You Like a Sister

"I'm not sure what it's for, but—"

"It was our wedding gift to you," Kayley said shyly.

"You guys got *me* a gift?" I asked, surprised.

"No!" Sammi said. "We *made* it for you. 'Cause you like homemade things."

I smiled. "That was a really great idea, Sammi."

"It wasn't her idea," Kayley corrected, "it was Cassie's."

I had passed surprised and was in the neighborhood of shocked. "Seriously?"

Cassie looked like she wanted to kill Kayley. She shrugged. "Whatever. You don't have to look like it's such a big deal, because it's not."

"I think it's a huge deal," I said quietly. "Especially the letters you guys wrote at the end."

Now Cassie was the one who looked like she wanted to disappear.

"Ever since I found out you guys existed, I've been trying so hard to get you to like me so I'd feel like I fit in," I confessed. "But every time I did that, it just backfired on me. And then when I decided to just be honest and be myself," I went on, with a glance at Cassie, "that's when things seemed to get better."

My dad nodded. "You can't go wrong with that."

"So, in the spirit of that, I just want to say that I honestly had no idea that the face mask was going to make our skin sting, or that the hair mask was going to turn your hair blue. And if you seriously think that I did, then you obviously don't know me like you think you do, and I'm not going to sit here apologizing and try and change your mind."

"I know you didn't know," Cassie said quietly.

A wave of relief washed over me. "Good. I'm glad." Okay, where was all this . . . *strength* coming from? This was so not me. But . . . maybe it *was* me, and it just hadn't had a chance to come out before.

"I really, really, *really* want to be you guys' sister—not your stepsister," I confessed. "And I hope you feel the same way, because if you don't, that's going to be really awkward."

Luckily, everyone laughed. It wasn't a big laugh—more like a nervous one—but it was something.

Like, maybe a start.

"I want that too!" Sammi yelled.

"Me too," Kayley added.

I smiled at them.

We all turned, waiting for Cassie.

"I do too," she finally said.

I didn't smile at her. I got up and went over and hugged her.

Because that's what sisters do.

Thirteen

♫

When Lana's hairdresser friend called back
later and had Lana read her all the ingredients in the
mask, she had no idea what could have made their
hair turn blue. Which meant she didn't have a sugges-
tion as to how to make it *un*blue, either. The fact that
the next day was Sunday, which meant that all the
hair salons were closed, didn't help things. Because it
was already midnight, Lana decided that we should
all go to sleep and maybe time would help somehow
and that another shower in the morning would take
care of things.

As she and Cassie showered at eight o'clock the

next morning, I made everyone a batch of my special chocolate chip pancakes. Because Mom wasn't there to be the sugar police, I was able to add as many chips as I wanted, which was about three quarters of the package.

"These are the BEST PANCAKES EVER!" Sammi shrieked as she ran around the table after finishing the one I had given her. I had tried to make it in the shape of Mickey Mouse, but instead it had resembled a camel.

"I'm glad you like them," I laughed.

Kayley gave up on using her fork and knife and decided to eat them like I usually did—reaching down and using a finger to scoop up the gooey chocolate. As I watched her, I smiled. It was nice to see her being so . . . *messy*. Maybe there was hope for her yet.

She looked up and stopped with her finger in mid-air. She looked so guilty you would have thought she had been caught robbing a bank. "Sorry. I don't know what I was thinking," she said as she quickly reached for her fork.

"Hopefully, you were thinking, *Avery's such a great*

cook I can't even bother to pick up a fork before I dig in!" I replied as I dipped my finger into my own pancake. "Not to brag, but I totally outdid myself with this batch."

She smiled and put down her fork. "Totally," she agreed as she followed my lead.

We were still eating (in addition to being delicious, the pancakes were also addictive) when Lana and Cassie came down a few minutes later with towels wrapped around their heads.

"Did it work?" I asked anxiously. I picked up the plates I had made for them. "Here—before you answer that, take these," I ordered as I held the pancakes out toward them. "No matter what, they'll make you feel better."

Lana and Cassie looked at each other and took off their towels.

My heart sank. "It's still blue," I sighed.

"I think it's actually *more* blue," Kayley said.

"Looks like there's going to be two other something blues in addition to the turtle," Lana said.

We turned to Cassie. I waited for her to freak out,

but instead she dug into her pancake and took a bite. "These are *good*," she said with her mouth full.

Huh. Maybe there was hope for all of us.

Lexi might have been a drama queen, but that wasn't always a bad thing. Because when things got crazy dramatic—like they did when you had blue hair on the day of a wedding—she had a knack for coming up with brilliant ideas.

Which was why I decided to call and fill her in on what was going on.

After a bunch of gasps and a few reactions of "YOU'VE GOT TO BE KIDDING!" and "That's INSANE!!!" I asked her if she had any ideas as to what we might do.

"I probably do, but I think before I share them, I should come over there so I can get a complete look at the situation," she replied.

Why did I know she was going to say that? That was another thing about Lexi—it wasn't good enough for her just to *hear* about drama. She had to be in the thick of it whenever possible.

"Well, sure, that would obviously be best," I said, half lying, "but I don't know how that's going to work, seeing that I'm at my dad's rather than at home."

"I'll call you right back," she said quickly, before hanging up.

Sure enough, she did. To share the news that her mom had agreed to drive her and she'd be there in a half hour.

"You guys are *sure* you want to do this?" Lana said later as we all crowded into her bathroom.

Me, Kayley, and Sammi nodded.

"It was Lexi's idea, and we think it's an awesome one," said Kayley.

"Thanks," Lexi said. "But when I come up with *really* awesome ones like this one, I feel like I can't totally take credit for them. It's almost like they're gifts from the universe, you know?"

"I really appreciate the sentiment, but having *all* of you have blue hair feels like a bit too much," Lana replied.

"But we're a *family*," I said. I looked at the clock.

"Or at least we will be in three hours. And this is what families do."

Lana thought about it and then hugged me. "We're already a family. It'll just be official as far as the law is concerned."

"I think it's a great idea," Cassie said.

"I'd do it too," Lexi offered. "Not that, you know, I was invited to the wedding," she replied. "Which I could totally still come to even if I were invited at the last minute, because I happen to be free this afternoon."

All I did was shake my head. There was too much going on for me to be embarrassed about what she was doing. I watched as Lana's lips twisted into a smile, which she quickly tried to get rid of. "I'm so glad to hear that," Lana said. "Because I think it would be wonderful if you could join us."

"For real?!" Lexi gasped.

Lana nodded.

"Awesome! Luckily, I already know what I'm going to wear."

Why did that not surprise me?

Lana picked up the tube of hair mask. "Well, if we're going to do this, we ought to get going."

I guess it would've looked strange if two members of a family had blue hair, but when an entire family did, it seemed kind of normal. Well, maybe if that family lived on another planet. But still.

At first my dad was a little hesitant about the idea, but when he saw how excited the three of us were about it, he agreed to go along. As Kayley shampooed the mask out of my hair in the sink, I got worried that maybe it wouldn't work—that for some reason my hair wouldn't change at all, or worse, it would turn pink or something—but once she said, "Okay—all done," and I popped my head up and looked in the mirror, I saw that I was safe. In this case, "safe" meant I had really, *really* blue hair. Sammi was so excited about the whole thing that she started begging Lana to let her keep her hair blue forever.

Mom and Lexi arrived at Cara Mia an hour before the ceremony was supposed to start, when me and the PFKABBs (People Formerly Known as BBs, as I couldn't really call them that anymore) were placing the mason jars full of tulips we had gotten at Trader Joe's around the dining room. (I had suggested the idea to Lana after seeing it on some HGTV decorating show about DIY weddings).

When she saw Lana, Mom's mouth twisted into a big O, which led me to believe that, for once, Lexi had actually kept a secret.

"Mom," I whispered, embarrassed, when she continued to stand there without moving.

"*Mom,*" I whispered again, this time louder.

"Have you posted a picture on Instagram yet?" Lexi asked. "You'll get so many regrams on it!"

"She's totally right," Cassie said, reaching for her phone and taking a selfie.

As Mom set up her camera gear, I filled her in on what had happened. By the end she couldn't stop laughing. Which, now that it was over, made me start laughing as well.

Mom hugged me. "How much do I love the fact that I have a daughter who is so lacking vanity she'd do that for someone?"

I cocked my head. "I'm not sure that's a compliment, Mom."

She kissed my cheek. "Oh, it is. Believe me."

When my dad and Lana walked in from the other room, Mom burst out laughing. "Sorry," she said through her giggles. "It's just . . . Matt, do you remember that time in college when you sprayed my Sun In in your hair by mistake?"

He squinted. "Oh yeah . . . ," he said as he remembered. He started to laugh. "I looked like Bozo the Clown."

Lana laughed too, but hers was a little too forced. "You never told me about that."

He shrugged. "I guess I had forgotten until right now." He smiled at Mom. "That was a funny time."

From the look on Lana's face, *that* was not what she wanted to hear. Mom noticed it too, because she immediately wiped the smile off her face. "Actually, it wasn't that funny," she said quickly.

"What are you talking about?" Dad asked. "Every time you thought about it for the next year, you'd laugh so hard you'd cry!"

Mom gave him the faintest shake of her head and motioned to Lana with her eyes. Finally he got it. "But thinking about it now, you're right. It was actually pretty stupid."

Lana didn't look convinced. "Excuse me for a second. I'm going to go . . . do something," she said, her voice wavering as she ran toward the other room.

Mom looked shocked. "I feel awful . . . I didn't mean . . ."

My dad waved her off. "It's not you. She's just been a little stressed the last few days. You know, the wedding and all . . ." He sounded like he was trying to convince himself just as much as her.

Mom nodded. "Right. Of course. Prewedding jitters." She didn't seem all that convinced either.

"I'll be right back," I announced. I glanced over at where Lexi was showing Cassie how to hold the camera for the best selfie angle, according to something she had read online by Kim Kardashian.

I headed to the bathroom and knocked on the door.

"I'll be out in a minute," Lana said, and sniffed. Her voice was all wavy, like she had been crying.

I had figured this was where she was hiding. Probably because the bathroom was where I hid when I was upset too. "It's Avery. Can I come in?"

"Oh. I . . . uh . . ."

I opened my bag and took out the emergency M&M'S I always carried with me. "I have chocolate."

The lock clicked open.

I slowly opened the door. "Hi."

She dabbed at her eyes with a tissue. "Hi," she said. "Allergies," she sniffled.

Yeah, right. I knew a fellow duck-and-crier when I saw one. I nodded. "I get them really bad too," I lied. I held out the M&M'S. "Want some?"

The words were barely out of my mouth before she snatched the package from me and ripped it open so fast that a bunch of the candies skittered across the floor.

"I'm such a mess!" she wailed.

"It's okay. They're only M&M'S."

She began to cry again.

"I can get more," I said nervously. "There's a convenience store across the street."

"I wasn't talking about that!" she wailed louder.

I started to panic. It had to be the hair thing. She had been acting like she was completely okay with walking down the aisle at her wedding with blue hair, but obviously that was just to make me feel better. "I'm so, so sorry, Lana," I said, tears welling up in my eyes. "I'd do anything to be able to fix your hair!"

She cried even more, which made *me* cry more.

"Why are you crying?" she asked through her tears.

"Because you're so upset about having blue hair!"

She shook her head. "That's not why I'm crying."

I stopped. "It's not?"

"No. I'm crying because . . ." She got more upset. "Oh, I feel so stupid!"

Okay, I knew that brides were known for being a little nutty, but this was entering a-*lot*-nuts territory.

"This is all just . . . so much," she confessed. "The move . . . trying to blend a family . . ." She sighed. "If you haven't noticed, I can be somewhat of a perfectionist."

"Really? Huh." I tried to look like that was news to me.

"And although I've been trying to keep it together, I think I'm just really . . . scared."

"Of what?"

"Everything," she said, throwing her hands up. She looked at me. "But mostly of letting you down."

"Me?" I asked, confused.

She nodded. "Yes. Before we got here, when I'd ask Matt about you—what you were like, what you liked—he never had a lot of answers. So I had this idea that you were just this average girl . . . but nothing could be further from the truth."

I wasn't sure if that was a good or bad thing.

"You're really incredible, Avery," she went on. "And I see the relationship you have with your mom, and how great it is, and I worry that you and I will never have that. I mean, I know I'm only your step-mother, so it's not like we're *supposed* to have that, but still—"

"Why can't we have that?" I asked. "I mean, I know when people hear the word 'stepmother,' they always think it's all negative. You know, like in fairy tales, but it doesn't *have* to be like that."

She smiled. "You're right. It doesn't."

"It just has to take time, is all." I smiled. "Time takes time."

"That's true." She nodded. "I like that."

"Thanks." I probably should've mentioned that I had stolen that from Dad, but it was such a nice moment. Why go and ruin it?

She opened her arms and hugged me. "I really lucked out getting you as part of this package."

I smiled. "Me too."

She let go and smoothed her dress. "We should get going. We have a wedding to put on."

And we did.

And although I hadn't been to very many in my life, I'd say it turned out to be a great one. No one tripped while walking down the aisle. No one flubbed the readings of the various poems that were part of the ceremony. No one bawled like a baby as Dad and Lana said their "I dos." (Okay, maybe I teared up a bit . . . or a bunch.) The food was great, and after we ate, even though there wasn't a lot of room, people moved the tables out of the way and made a little dance floor, and Mom ran out to her car and rummaged through her trunk and found her iPhone speakers, and everyone danced, even my grandparents. (That alone was worth all of it—to see two old people jumping around to Taylor Swift's "Shake It Off.")

After we had the cake, Dad and Lana gave a speech about how much it meant to them that everyone was there, and how it had been the perfect afternoon. Dad even said that he was thinking of permanently keeping his hair blue, which got a big laugh.

"And now we'd like to invite anyone who might have a few words they'd like to say to come up and share," Dad said when the laughter had died down.

I looked over toward my grandmother. She always had *something* to add, but this time she stayed quiet. In fact, everyone did. And then—completely surprising myself—I felt my hand shoot up.

"I'd like to say something," I said.

What was I doing?! I hated speaking in public!

Dad smiled. "Great. Come on up."

Before I knew it, I was on my feet, making my way

up to the microphone. As I looked out at the crowd, I felt myself start to sweat, praying that they couldn't see it.

I cleared my throat. "Hi. For those of you who don't know me, I'm, um, Avery." I glanced over at the BBs. "And those girls over there"—I motioned—"they're my . . . *sisters*."

At that mention of the word "sisters," not only did they smile, but so did my parents—all three of them.

"We actually haven't known each other for that long, but in the short time that we have, we've kind of been through a lot." At that, Cassie gave a little nod.

"My mom likes to say that while you don't get to pick your family, you do get to pick your friends." I turned toward Lexi. "And I've been really lucky that I've picked awesome ones," I said as she got all teary. "But in this case, I'm extra lucky that even if these people weren't my family, I'd be really honored to call them my friends."

My speech went on, but I don't really remember what I said. I was too busy smiling at them.

IF YOU ♥ THIS BOOK,
you'll love all the rest from

YOUR HOME AWAY FROM HOME:

AladdinMix.com

HERE YOU'LL GET:

- ♥ The first look at new releases
- ♥ Chapter excerpts from all the Aladdin M!X books
- ♥ Videos of your fave authors being interviewed